The Marriage Tree

W.J. EATON

The Marriage Tree
Copyright © 2019 by W.J. Eaton. All rights reserved.

No part of this publication may be reproduced, stored in a retrieval system or transmitted in any way by any means, electronic, mechanical, photocopy, recording or otherwise without the prior permission of the author except as provided by USA copyright law.

The opinions expressed by the author are not necessarily those of URLink Print and Media.

1603 Capitol Ave., Suite 310 Cheyenne, Wyoming USA 82001
1-888-980-6523 | admin@urlinkpublishing.com

URLink Print and Media is committed to excellence in the publishing industry.

Book design copyright © 2019 by URLink Print and Media. All rights reserved.

Published in the United States of America

ISBN 978-1-64753-125-6 (Paperback)
ISBN 978-1-64753-124-9 (Digital)

27.11.19

CONTENTS

Prologue 7
Chapter 1: The Encounter 9
Chapter 2: Growing Unrest 12
Chapter 3: First Blood 15
Chapter 4: Brother Against Brother 19
Chapter 5: Return To The Farm 24
Chapter 6: Under The Marriage Tree 29
Chapter 7: Wanderings 35
Chapter 8: Stonewall Falls 42
Chapter 9: Gettysburg 48
Chapter 10: Father Abraham 53
Chapter 11: Four Score 59
Chapter 12: John Wilkes Booth 65
Chapter 13: Re-Election 73
Chapter 14: Surrender 80
Chapter 15: Sic Semper Tyrannis 89
Chapter 16: Fallen Cold And Dead 96
Chapter 17: Carpetbaggers And Scalawags 107
Epilogue 117

PROLOGUE

Evangeline suddenly became aware that she was flushed and sweating in the attic. When she had begun to go through the old books, it had been light out but the sun had not yet risen above the horizon. She knew she would soon have to go downstairs and get out of the heat. She was about to do so when she pulled some smaller books off the deep shelves. When she did, she realized that behind them had been hidden a miniature chest.

She was very curious as to what she would find inside. She thought it might be locked, but it was not. She opened it slowly and discovered a stack of old letters. She was excited about what these were and forgot about the heat. She opened the one on top and began to read it. She was stunned. It was a letter her husband Liam had written to her before they had been married. She and her husband were only married a short time because he had been killed during the war between North and South. She had long ago forgotten about these letters. She wondered how they had gotten on these shelves in this chest. She finished the first letter and opened the second one. It was another one from her husband to her. She read that one, then another. She was overwhelmed with joy and then became pensive. She stopped and walked over to one of the attic windows. She had always liked the view from the attic of the creek bordering her husband's family farm. . .

1

THE ENCOUNTER

*L*iam sat looking out over the water, as the sun reflecting off the water stared back at him. It was so bright he had to shade his eyes. It was hot and he was fatigued from running around in the heat. His mind wandered, as it so often did. He imagined the life that the wide creek before him had sustained in times past and as he did, a bald eagle flew high overhead, riding the air currents above. He drifted deeper into his musings and thought of himself as a Nanticoke Indian. Their presence had seldom been witnessed for a long time. Most had moved into Delaware which saddened Liam. His young mind understood the injustice of it and was sickened by it... Exploitation of other people was wrong. *Why couldn't everyone see that*, he thought. He was so happy that his family had freed old Samuel years before. He had heard his father talk about tensions between free and slave states. Maryland was actually intensely divided on the issue. Officially, Maryland was a slave state, but about half of its slaves had been freed. Liam felt sure that the slavery issue would tear America apart . . .

Liam was interrupted from his thoughts by a rustling in the grass. He looked up to see a young girl running away from where he sat. Her hair was wet and she had obviously been in the creek. He had never seen her before. He called out to her, "Hi there. I'm Liam. What's your name?"

She stopped and looked around. Liam thought she had the face of an angel.

"I'm Evangeline," she replied.

Liam thought she also had a beautiful name. What he was feeling, he had never felt before. He had never really paid much attention to girls. After all he was only 10, and girls had always seemed so boring. This one, however, for some reason interested him very much. "I've never seen you before, Evangeline. Did you just move here?"

"My family bought the farm across the creek from here. We moved in yesterday. It's so hot. I wanted to cool off, so I went for a swim in the creek. I came ashore down below here."

Liam was not sure what to say next. "Welcome. Do you have to go home right away? Do you think we could talk some more? Or, maybe we could play."

Evangeline smiled what Liam thought was the most radiant smile he had ever seen.

"I could stay for a while."

Liam's heart felt like it had jumped up into his throat. He said, "Come over into the shade of the tree with me. It's much cooler there."

She followed and sat down next to him. They talked some more, and then she looked up into the tree. "Liam, do see that? Two of the branches high up on this tree are connected to both trunks! I've never seen that before."

"I've never noticed that before. That's very interesting."

A bell began to ring. "Oh," said Evangeline, "that's my dinner bell. I have to go home now."

Liam said, "Will I see you tomorrow?"

"Maybe," she said, and ran off.

Liam smiled and he followed her with his eyes till she was out of sight. He was not sure what he was feeling. All he knew was that it felt good. He slowly started walking toward his own home. He was in no hurry. He wanted to savor the moment. He knew he had to see Evangeline again. He knew he would and would somehow make sure that their paths crossed again.

2

GROWING UNREST

Liam saw Evangeline a few times afterward. Then tensions over the slavery issue caused his and Evangeline's families to no longer associate with each other. His family thought slavery should be abolished while Evangeline's felt it should continue. Liam and Evangeline were devastated. They so desired to continue to see each other. But about a year and a half had passed without that happening. Yet Liam could not forget his friend nor did he have any intention of doing so. He wanted to see her, even if she agreed with her family that slavery was not wrong. *What would he do, though, if that was the way she felt?* He didn't know, but they would make it work. He knew they could. He began to plan to see her.

Two nights later on a moonless night, he swam across the creek, crawled up onto the shore behind Evangeline's house, and made his way around the house to below where her bedroom window was. An ivy vine covered the wall on that side. Liam grabbed onto it and began to climb to the second floor. When he reached Evangeline's window to his left, he tapped lightly on it with his knuckles. At first there was no response. He waited for a minute with great anticipation. Then Evangeline's face appeared. Her eyes widened and she gave him a broad smile. She opened the window and he crawled into her bedroom. "Liam, I don't believe you came here, but I'm so glad to see you! If father finds you are here, he'll have you shot."

Liam took both of her hands in his. "I don't care. I had to see you. I've missed you so much!"

"I've missed you, too, but it's really dangerous for you to be here."

"Will you leave with me now so we can spend some time together?" he replied.

"I don't know. I'm scared."

"Do you trust me, Evangeline?"

"Well, yes I do, Liam."

"Then come with me. We have to talk."

"Okay. Then turn around so I can change."

Liam allowed her to get ready, then she slipped out her window and they descended to the ground. Evangeline followed him, and they both ran off into the night. When they arrived at a little grove, they stopped. They both sat down in the cool, damp grass. For a while all that could be heard was their labored breathing. As that faded, Liam broke the silence. "Evangeline, I need to know what you believe about slavery. I know what your family's stance is. Your father has made it very clear. Do you agree with him?"

"Liam, I love my family very much, but I don't believe that slavery is right. In fact it does not seem to fit with our religious beliefs at all. I've been secretly reading *Uncle Tom's Cabin*. It's the story of a Christian slave. It exposes the horrific treatment that slaves encounter every day. The images the book presents have actually been preying on my mind. I've had bad dreams."

"What do you think we can do?"

"I've tried to talk to my father. He just is not going to let his slaves go. He's become very wealthy by their backbreaking work."

"I wish we were older, so our elders would listen to us. I feel we have no voice."

"I agree, Liam. But count your blessings, your father has freed his slaves."

After their conversation Liam took Evangeline back home. They snuck away to be together often in the following years. They were never caught by their parents. Evangeline said it was providence. She felt God wanted them to be together, so they could support each other.

As the years passed and they matured into young adulthood, they witnessed many other developments that led their nation into increasing turmoil. First, the Kansas Nebraska Act was passed. It overturned the Missouri Compromise and opened up the Northern Territories to slavery. It infuriated abolitionists. About three years later, the Dred Scott case reached the Supreme Court. The justices ruled that slaves could not be considered citizens. They also ruled that slaveholders could take existing slaves into slave-free areas of the country. This also angered abolitionists. Approximately two years after that, John Brown attacked Harper's Ferry, raiding the armory there. His plan was to start a slave uprising. Brown and two Negroes were hanged. Then maybe the most significant event as far as many Southerners were concerned took place— Abraham Lincoln was elected the 16th President of the United States. The South hated him. After he won the election, Southern states began seceding from the nation. The countdown to conflict had begun.

3

FIRST BLOOD

Though several Southern states had seceded because of the election of Abraham Lincoln, he was not yet in office when war broke out between the North and South. James Buchanan was still President when the Confederates began bombing Fort Sumter in Charlestown harbor in South Carolina. The thundering of their artillery sounded the bell of war in the United States. The time for negotiating was past. The militaries of both sides would speak for them from that point for four years.

Fortunately, the assault on the fort brought about no loss of life in the fledgling conflict. That would happen five days later in Baltimore. A riot broke out between Confederate sympathizers and members of the Massachusetts militia that was on its way to Washington, D.C., to join the war effort. The mob of sympathizers subsequently attacked the rear companies of the militia. The Union soldiers fired into the crowd, killing 12 civilians. Four of the soldiers also were killed. A brawl between the two sides and the Baltimore police ensued. Martial law in Baltimore was enforced about a month later. The riot further forced both sides to take a strong stance. By the summer of 1861, thousands of Marylanders sympathetic toward the South had crossed the Potomac into Virginia to fight for the Confederacy.

One of those that left Maryland to join the Southern forces was Evangeline's brother, Ewell. She and her mother begged him not to go. He was only 22. His father encouraged him to go. Evangeline's parents didn't speak to each other for weeks afterward. Evangeline cried for two days.

On the other side of the conflict, Liam asked permission to join the Union forces. His mother was completely against it. His father said it was Liam's decision since he was 21. Liam enlisted soon thereafter. He knew he would have to tell Evangeline. He knew she would be upset. He also knew he couldn't live with himself if he didn't fight for what he believed. He hadn't seen Evangeline since before Fort Sumter had been attacked. He started to make plans to see her. He also became more determined to marry her. They had talked about it several times. He felt she would be better protected by the North's forces. He thought that the Union would have a quick victory over the Confederates. He couldn't bear the thought of her being mistreated if she were on the losing side.

The night before he was planning on enlisting, he swam across the creek to Evangeline's home. He climbed the ivy as he had so many times before and tapped on her bedroom window pane. She came to the window, opened it, and kissed him. "I've missed you so much, Liam. I love you so much!"

"I love you, too. Come with me. We have to talk."

"Let me get changed. I'll only be a minute."

Quickly they were out her window and running away from her house. Evangeline started to head toward their usual spot on her side of the creek. Liam grabbed her hand. "No, come this way."

She ran with him but looked puzzled when they reached the shore of the creek. "Liam, where are you taking me?"

"We're going across the creek."

"Why would we go over there?"

"I want to marry you. Reverend Crane's waiting for us by the tree where we first met. That's where we should be married."

"How can we be married? There's a war and our families are on opposite sides. My brother has already gone to Virginia to enlist."

Liam suddenly had a concerned look. "I'm so sorry to hear that, Evangeline."

Evangeline knew something was really wrong. "What is it, Liam? You're not telling me something."

"I'm going to join the Union Army tomorrow."

"What? Are you crazy?"

"I have to fight for what I believe."

"What about me? I could lose a brother and the one I love."

"I don't believe the war will last long. There won't be much fighting."

"Liam, what if you're wrong? How can I marry you if you're going off to war?"

"I'm sure I'm right. Will you marry me tonight?"

"You expect me to swim across the creek and get married soaking wet?"

"I love you dry or wet, Evangeline."

"That's what I love about you. You're the most complex simple man that I know. Yes, I will marry you!"

"Let's go, then! The Reverend's waiting."

They waded out into the creek together and then swam side by side to the opposite shore. When they arrived on the other side, Reverend Crane was waiting for them. He greeted them with a smile. "I wondered when this day would come. I've watched your friendship blossom into love. That's the only reason I've agreed to do this."

"Thank you, Reverend Crane. You don't know what this means to us," Liam replied. "You'll see to it that she is well cared for, won't you?"

"Of course I will. I know this will cause her father and maybe the rest of her family to disown her."

With that Reverend Crane performed their wedding ceremony. He asked them if they had rings. Evangeline had had no time to purchase one, but Liam had gotten a thin silver band for her. He slid it on her finger and they kissed.

Reverend Crane said, "Come with me."

They followed him to his parsonage. "I've set up the guest room for you two tonight."

"Thank you so much," they responded together. Liam picked her up and carried her into the room. He kicked the door shut with his heel.

The next morning Reverend Crane sent Evangeline away to a widow he knew. After kissing his bride, Liam, determined to be true to his convictions, headed off to fight for the freedom of men and women he didn't know.

4

BROTHER AGAINST BROTHER

*L*iam was glad that the time of training had been completed. He knew he needed to learn how to fight, but he was anxious to make a difference for his country. He wanted to help ensure that what was good about America remained. The first decisive conflict of the Eastern Theater of the war, the First Battle of Bull Run had been fought the previous summer. It was an important Confederate victory. He felt that the next one would happen soon. He was ready to join the fight. It was good that his unit was finally on the move. They were marching into Virginia. He prayed for a Union victory.

He finally saw action on May 23, 1862, at Front Royal, Virginia. His regiment, the 1st Maryland, had been assigned to Major General Nathaniel Banks in March of 1862 and had made its way into the Shenandoah Valley. Under General Banks, the regiment of about 9,000 men settled themselves in and north of the town. Banks had placed two companies at the Buckton Depot under Colonel John Kenly on May 22nd. The next day Major General Jackson, commanding the Confederate Army of the Valley, marched to within 10 miles of the town.

On the 23rd the Louisiana "Tigers," who were known for being fearless and hard fighting, and the Maryland 1st, CSA attacked the Union forces at the depot, overrunning it. Kenly and his men, which included the Union Maryland 1st, then began retreating through the town, fighting as they went. As Liam and the men with him ducked behind buildings or other objects, they returned fire on the enemy. This went on for some time, seemingly intensifying as it continued. Bullets were whizzing all around Liam. He would run and then get behind something for cover. Then he would load his rifle and shoot at the enemy. It was very tight quarters and made it difficult to make accurate shots. Liam was beginning to tire and slid between two buildings to catch his breath. He loaded his gun and waited. He shot and felled a Confederate. He loaded his gun again and started to retreat again. As he was backing his way through the streets, he saw Ewell, Evangeline's brother. He aimed his rifle to shoot, but he couldn't. Then his and Ewell's eyes met for a couple seconds. "Traitor!" yelled Ewell. He pulled the trigger of his gun and shot Liam in the chest. Liam fell to the ground, thinking of his Evangeline, and died. Ewell, filled with hatred, kicked Liam's body a couple of times to make sure he was dead. Then he moved on to continue fighting, leaving Liam lying there in the dirt. Liam had been right. His time to fight was short . . .

Evangeline held her beautiful baby girl. She had named her Hope. Hope had been born shortly after Evangeline had received a letter from Liam. Liam had written that his unit was about to leave for Virginia. Evangeline had named her Hope, because she was ever hopeful that Liam would return home. She wanted the one she loved to see his daughter. She expected that Liam didn't know he was a father. Hope began to cry and Evangeline held her closer. She began rocking her baby in her arms. Hope soon began to whimper and then fell asleep. Evangeline put her in her crib. She went out to the living room of Mrs. Dodd's house and sat down by a light to read the paper. There was an article in it concerning the Union war effort in the Eastern Theater to that point. She read about how at the start of the war the Confederates had the edge in victories, but that in recent months the Union seemed to be turning the tide. This gave her much encouragement. She hoped the fighting would soon cease. She missed Liam terribly. It was difficult caring for a child by herself. Mrs. Dodd had been very supportive of her and the baby's needs, but Hope needed her father in her life.

Months went by and Evangeline hadn't heard anything from Liam. As the days continued to pass, she began to become alarmed and worried ceaselessly. She couldn't sleep and was having difficulty caring for Hope. Mrs. Dodd helped all she could, but she knew that the baby needed a mother focused on her baby. So one night after Evangeline had put the baby down, Mrs. Dodd took her by the hand and sat her on the couch. "Honey, we need to talk. I know you're worried about your husband, but you have a child to take care of. I'm trying to help all I can, but I'm no substitute for you. You're both suffering because of your inattentiveness. I know what you're going through. My husband died when he was young and left me with three children. They needed me. I didn't have time to fret over the fact that he was gone. I had to work and I had to take care of my children. I know it's hard when you don't know. But I can tell you that if you pay attention to your baby as you should, it will help the time pass till you know your husband's circumstances."

Evangeline stared blankly for a few moments and then burst into tears. "I'm so afraid he's gone. What'll I do if he doesn't return? I can't go back to my family. Even my mother disowned me."

"Honey, you have me. I'm not going anywhere. That's more than I had. You can stay here as long as you like. You'll make it no matter what happens. Now why don't you go to bed? You look exhausted. We can talk more in the morning."

Evangeline was not only very tired but also depressed. She knew Mrs. Dodd was right. She needed to get her rest; she needed to focus on her little girl. She would leave Liam in God's hands. After all, hadn't she been praying for him ceaselessly? What more could she do for him so far away?

The next morning Evangeline awoke to the crying of her baby. She was feeling much better. She got up and picked up her baby and cradled her in her arms. She fed Hope and played with her for a while. Then she put her down for a short nap. After Hope woke, Evangeline decided she was going to go for a walk. She told Mrs. Dodd where she was going and stepped out into the sunlight. It was very bright and already quite warm. As she was walking along the street, she saw someone she knew and did not expect to see. Reverend Crane was walking toward her. Her heart sank. She stopped and let him come to her.

"Hello, Evangeline."

She knew by the look on his face that the news wasn't good. She could barely talk. "Reverend Crane, I know. I don't want to know what you have to say." Her lips began to quiver.

"Liam is gone, Evangeline. He died at the Battle of Front Royal on May 23rd."

Sobbing now, Evangeline said, "How'd you find out?"

"I received two letters from your cousin, Bo. He sent them to me, because he knew I knew your whereabouts. Liam had told him. Liam had given him a letter he had written before he died. He made Bo promise to get it to you if he was killed. The second letter is from Bo. It explains how Liam was killed. I read it because it was addressed to me. I must tell you that it's shocking."

"I don't want to read them here. I need time. Will you come back to the house with me? Mrs. Dodd'll be happy to see you. Maybe we can all have lunch."

"Sure, Evangeline, I'll be glad to come with you."

And she and the Reverend walked back to Mrs. Dodd's house. When they arrived, she went in first and called out, "Mrs. Dodd, Reverend Crane's here."

Mrs. Dodd entered the living room from the kitchen. She knew by the look on Evangeline's face that the news wasn't good. "Hello, Reverend Crane."

"Good morning, Mrs. Dodd."

"If you'll excuse me, I'm going to go to my room with Hope." Then Evangeline turned and went to her room. Once there, she held the baby in one arm and read Liam's letter. He had received hers! She started to cry. *He knew he was a father before he died.* That made her very happy. She read on and he explained that they were on the march, and that they would probably see battle soon. He closed, telling her he loved her and missed her so much. She began sobbing again. When she had regained her composure, she unfolded the second letter. Her cousin Bo related how the Confederates had driven their unit from the depot they were guarding. He told how they retreated and fought within the town's streets. Then he revealed that he saw who killed Liam: her brother Ewell! She screamed, "How could he? I'll forever hate him!"

5

RETURN TO THE FARM

It had been less than a month after Evangeline's learning of Liam's death that she received word from her mother that Ewell had been severely injured. Her mother had asked her to return to the family farm to see him, because his condition had been worsening and recovery from his wounds seemed unlikely. When Evangeline first got the letter, she furiously tore it up. Then she prayed that the Lord would forgive her. After that she began to pray for her brother, and though she had not forgiven him, she decided she must make the trip to her home. Five days later, she was on her way with little Hope.

When she arrived at the farm, her mother greeted her warmly. She didn't want to let go of her daughter or granddaughter. As she was hugging them, Evangeline's father entered the room. He stared coldly at Evangeline and Hope. "You can stay here long enough to pay respects to your brother, then you and that child must leave. You're no longer my daughter, and she's the daughter of a traitor," her father stated flatly.

It was all Evangeline could do to hold her tongue. But she did and walked away from her father without a word. Her mother led her to where her brother was being kept.

When she saw him, she was horrified. His left leg and arm were gone. He looked up at her with a faint smile when she entered the room. "Hi, Evangeline," he said.

"Hello, Ewell."

"I don't think I'm going to make it, Sis. They can't keep the infection from these wounds under control. I'm glad you came. I must talk to you. Mother, can you leave us?" With that their mother turned and left the room. "I'm like this because of what I did, Sis. This happened to me at the Battle of Malvern Hill. I was hit by artillery. It's retribution for what I did at Front Royal. You see, Liam saw me on the battlefield and had me in his sights, but he couldn't shoot me. I should just have left him there, but I aimed my rifle and shot him in the chest. He died quickly. I'm so sorry. I didn't know he was your husband." He began crying. After he somewhat composed himself, he said, "Mom and dad didn't tell me till I returned home. There's no excuse for what I did, but I would've passed him by had I known. Can you forgive me?"

Evangeline turned her face away from him and prayed silently, *Lord, help me.* "I didn't think I could, Ewell, but yes, I can forgive you." At that moment something happened in her heart, and she determined to try to reconcile Liam's and her family. She and her brother talked a while longer. He told her about the other battles that he fought in: the First Battle of Winchester, the Battle of Cross Keys, the Battle of Gaines Mill, and finally, the Battle of Malvern Hill. He related to her the horrible carnage he had seen. Then she rose, kissed him on the forehead, and left the room. Her mother was holding and rocking little Hope. She walked over to where her mother was sitting and took Hope from her mother's arms. "Mother, I have forgiven Ewell."

Her mother began to cry. "Oh, dear, I'm so glad! This family has been torn apart since that war began. I would love you to stay with us, but your stubborn father will not allow it."

"Mother, what do you think the chances are of our family being one again?"

"Slim to not at all, I believe. Your father's very bitter."

"Pray that we will be, mother. I believe God will do the rest." As she said it, though, she doubted. Liam had thought the war would be short and that he would come home soon. Neither of those things was going to happen. She wondered whether God was really in control. She wasn't sure anymore if he cared. "I'm going to go now. I don't know if I'll return. That's up to father." She and her mother hugged and kissed, and her mother kissed little Hope. Then Evangeline left. She slowly walked several blocks to her friend Rachel's house where she had made arrangements to stay for the night.

The next morning as she and Rachel were having tea, there was knock at the door. Rachel went and opened it. Evangeline's mother entered. "Darling, what have you decided?" she asked.

"I told you yesterday that that depends on father."

"I'm sorry to say that he has not changed his mind about you staying at the house, but he now has no problem with you staying in town. Will you stay so I can see you and my granddaughter?"

Evangeline considered this for a minute and answered, "I'll stay. But be sure that I'm going to Liam's parents while I'm here. Hope is their granddaughter too."

Her mother replied, "I understand. I'll stay in touch."

"What's father going to say about you seeing me?"

"Don't worry about that, Evangeline, my dear. He can't prevent me from doing something he doesn't know anything about." She and Evangeline hugged and she left.

The baby began to cry, and Evangeline changed and fed her. Then she purposed to go to Liam's parents. She dressed the baby and borrowed Rachel's carriage to make the trip. After about a 15 minute trip she arrived at the Conroy's farm.

She wondered what kind of a reception she would receive from them. She didn't even know if they knew that she and Liam had married. She stopped the carriage, tied it up at a post, and got off of it. With Hope in her arms she went to the front door and knocked.

Mrs. Conroy came to the door. "Evangeline, what are you doing here?"

"Can I come in?"

"Of course you can, Evangeline."

"I have something I must tell you. Is Mr. Conroy here?"

"He's out in the field."

"Can you call him in Mrs. Conroy?"

"Sure, let me go get him." With that she got up and went outside. She returned several minutes later with her husband. They came into the living room and both of them sat down.

"What do you want to tell us?" Mr. Conroy asked.

"Do you know about Liam?"

"What about Liam?" Mrs. Conroy asked. "We've not heard from him since he wrote about his training."

"You don't know. Liam was killed in action during the Battle of Front Royal."

Mrs. Conroy burst into tears and Mr. Conroy turned ashen.

"I have more to tell you. Before Liam went off to war, we were secretly married under that old, strange tree down by the creek. You know, the one with the two trunks that are joined by two branches. On our honeymoon night, I conceived. This little girl is our daughter and your granddaughter. I thought you should know. I'll leave if you want me to."

"Leave, heavens no, my child, please stay." Mrs. Conroy wiped her tears away with her kerchief. "Can I hold the child? What's her name?"

"Her name's Hope. I named her that in the hope that Liam would return home safely. I loved him so much. I really miss him!" She began sobbing.

Mrs. Conroy grabbed her husband's hand and squeezed it. "We'll miss him, too. Just be sure you can count on us to be there for you." Mr. Conroy nodded his head yes in affirmation. Mrs. Conroy said, "We haven't seen you in a long time. Are you going to stay in town? Are you going to stay with your parents?"

"I can't. My father has disowned me."

"Then stay with us," Mrs. Conroy replied. "I'll get the guest room ready."

6

UNDER THE MARRIAGE TREE

The next few weeks spent with the Conroys were wonderful for Evangeline. Mr. and Mrs. Conroy treated her like she was their daughter. They spent a lot of time with Hope, which truly blessed Evangeline. During those same weeks, her mother visited frequently. If her father knew about those visits, her mother wasn't letting on that he did. She reflected often on how hard it was for her mother to have to deal with her father's bitterness and anger, and how it was dividing their family. Unfortunately, this divisiveness reached a new level of intensity the day her brother, Ewell died. Her mother came over to the Conroy's that day, crying uncontrollably. It took Evangeline and Mrs. Conroy about 20 minutes to get her calmed down enough that she could speak to them.

"I'm beside myself, honey. I don't know what to do! I'm trying to mourn your brother's death, and I have to deal with your father. If his anger doesn't kill him, I'm afraid it's going to kill me."

"Mother, I've been praying. Have you?"

"No, I'm sorry to say I haven't. I'm unable to focus. Forgive me."

"I forgive you," Evangeline tenderly replied. "But you need to stay with me here. This has gone on long enough. You and I need to go and confront father."

"I'm frightened, dear. I'm terrified that he may kill you and maybe me in his rage. He carries a gun all the time now."

"We have God, mother. David went up against Goliath with five smooth stones. Goliath had a sword and spear, but he was felled by a boy with a sling and a stone. You have nothing to fear. Even if father should kill us both, we would go to heaven to be with the Lord. Do you believe that?"

"Yes, I do."

"Then you and I are going to get back in your carriage and go to the farm. Mrs. Conroy may I leave Hope with you?"

"Yes, Evangeline, you can. I'll take good care of her. I'll be praying for both of you."

"Thank you," said Evangeline. "We're going to need it."

Evangeline took her mother by the hand and led her to the carriage. She took the reins and shook them to get the horse moving. The short trip in the carriage was a silent one. She prayed for her mother and herself. She knew she had a battle on her hands. She knew she needed the Lord's wisdom, words, and strength. Her mother needed courage, and she interceded that the Lord would provide it. As she pulled up to the front of the house, she saw her father on the porch with his rifle.

"Martha, what're you doing with that woman? Get out of that carriage and go into the house. I'll deal with you later. And you, get out of my carriage and walk away."

Evangeline grabbed her mother's arm. "Stay here. Father, I'm not going anywhere. We're going to have a talk." She jumped down out of the carriage, still holding her mother's arm. As her feet touched the ground, a bullet kicked up dust in front of them.

"I've warned you. You let go of my wife's arm! You take another step closer and I'll kill you!"

Evangeline felt the Spirit was holding her in place. She didn't let go of her mother's arm, nor did she take another step.

At the same time her father's hardness seemed to soften a little. "Don't call me father. I have nothing to say to you."

"You're going to hear me out," said Evangeline. "This has got to stop! You're tearing what's left of our family apart. I'm not going to stand back and watch it any longer. I've lost my husband."

"He was a traitor to the South!"

"I won't have you talk about him like that! I've lost him, and my brother— your son, killed him. He asked me to forgive him and I did. If I can do that, you can too."

"I can't forgive Union sympathizers!"

"That may be so, but tomorrow at three o'clock you'll get your chance. I'm staying at the Conroy's farm. We'll be waiting for you and mother under the tree where Liam and I were married."

Her father answered sternly, "I'll be there, but it won't be to talk! Someone's going to die!"

Evangeline let go of her mother's arm and watched her run into the house. Then she turned to go, never looking back. She had opened the door to reconciliation. The rest would be up to God. She was glad that it was in His hands. She walked back to the Conroy's farm. Upon her arrival, Mr. and Mrs. Conroy met her on their porch. "How did it go, Evangeline?" Mr. Conroy asked.

"Not well. Father's so angry. I'm not sure what he'll do to my mother. His hatred has completely blinded him. I don't think you two should go to the tree tomorrow. I'm afraid he might shoot you."

"Don't worry, sweetheart, we're committed to this and we trust God," answered Mr. Conroy.

"You're right," Evangeline replied. "We're all in God's hands. I'm tired. I'm going to take a nap while the baby's sleeping." She went into her bedroom, kissed her daughter on the forehead, and lay down on her bed. She fell asleep and dreamed she was with Liam. They were running across the field of his farm together, hand in hand. They finally stopped under the tree where they were married. They lay down in the grass together and he held her tight. Then he said to her, "This tree is a source of joy for you and I, but one day it'll bring much sorrow." She abruptly awoke to Hope crying. It was twilight and her baby was hungry. She fed her and then moved to the living room. The Conroys sat on either side of her, and she told them her dream. Then the conversation turned to memories of Liam , , ,

The next morning they were all up early. Mr. Conroy had breakfast and went out into the fields to work until the meeting. Evangeline fed Hope and she and Mrs. Conroy talked more about Liam. Finally, the time came to go to the tree. It was within walking distance, so they made their way across a field to it. They arrived there early and waited for Evangeline's father and mother to appear. The time seemed to pass agonizingly slowly. At last she could see her parents' carriage rolling toward them. As they pulled up, she was shocked to see that her mother's face was bruised. And her father was carrying his pistol.

"What have you done? I don't believe you've hit mother!"

"Shut up, woman! I told you there was going to be trouble!" He pushed his wife out of the carriage onto the ground and pulled out his revolver. He aimed it at Mr. Conroy, then Mrs. Conroy, and lastly at Evangeline. His eyes narrowed and he started to pull the trigger when Evangeline's mother jumped up and grabbed him by the leg, throwing him off balance. The gun went off harmlessly into the air. He dropped to the ground and took aim again. Just as he pulled the trigger, his wife stepped in front of him and was shot in the chest. She fell against him and he stepped back, wide-eyed with terror. He turned to run, but Mr. Conroy tackled him and took away his pistol and pointed it at him. "Get up and turn around," Mr. Conroy said. "Get a piece of rope out of his carriage and tie him up, Evangeline."

"What about mother?"

"I'm afraid she's dead."

Evangeline took the rope to Mr. Conroy, and Mr. Conroy had his wife hold the gun on Evangeline's father as he tied him up. As he did so, Evangeline knelt on the ground next to her mother and wept . . .

Three days later Evangeline's mother was buried. Her father was arrested, tried, and found guilty of manslaughter. He was sentenced to six years in prison. The fact that he had beaten his wife prior to her death added time to his sentence. Evangeline went to see him once, and found a broken shell of a man that just stared into space. She wept and was angry about how her family had been destroyed by the war. She had suffered three deaths of loved ones, and for all intents and purposes, her father was as good as dead. All she had left was her little Hope. She thanked God for that. She was so fed up with the evil the war had caused in general and to her specifically. She wanted to do something about it. But what could she do? She spent the next few months living with the Conroys and praying for an answer. Though all of her family but her daughter was gone, God gave her the grace to make the most of each day. She thanked God continuously for her in-laws and the opportunity to really get to know them. She came to love them deeply and trusted them completely. As she came to the full realization of this, she began to believe that the Lord was prompting her to leave her daughter with

Liam's parents where she would be safe. She wasn't sure what to do, but she felt the Lord would show her in his time. It would be so hard to leave her daughter. She knew that her in-laws would take good care of Hope, but she had to be sure that what she was thinking was correct. She continued to pray for guidance.

7

WANDERINGS

*E*vangeline continued to pray and reflect over the next few weeks. She was feeling an increasingly great need to do something to put an end to all of the bloodshed. Many lives had been lost over the recent months as the North and South continued to engage each other in the Eastern Theater. A major confrontation had taken place at Winchester, resulting in a Confederate victory. A second major battle had also been fought at Manassas. That was also a Confederate victory. It seemed as though Lee and Jackson could not be stopped. The Battle of Antietam took place a little over two weeks later. McClellan finally was able to put an end to Lee's push into the North. That was welcome relief for the Union, but it came at a very high cost for both sides. The carnage that she had read about reminded her of Revelation, and blood flowing as high as horses' bridles. It truly seemed as though America was in the middle of an apocalypse. She began to wonder how a fight over slavery had morphed into the all out war it was becoming. Why would families and friends tear each other apart, as she had witnessed firsthand? She decided that it was time to talk to the Conroys but held off doing so for another two days. Autumn was well underway and winter would not be far behind. She thought that maybe that would bring a natural break to the bloodshed. Maybe she should wait and spend a few more months with her daughter... Hope began to cry and she got up and fed her. Then she cradled her in her arms and rocked her, looking into her beautiful little face. She would wait... for now.

More minor engagements continued to take place throughout the fall and into winter. So Evangeline vacillated between staying with her daughter and seeking a way to make a difference for almost another three months. Then another major confrontation occurred at Fredericksburg. This resulted in another Confederate victory. Evangeline suddenly realized that she had been holding on too strongly to Liam's dream of a short war. She knew that wasn't going to be the case. The time for action had come.

The next morning she awoke early and fed Hope. She was going to have a long day. She needed to make the most of her time. She went out to the kitchen and found Mr. and Mrs. Conroy sitting at the table eating breakfast. "I need to talk to you, mom and dad." She had been calling them that for a while. It seemed so natural. They had become her mother and father. "I have been wrestling with something for a long while."

"We know, dear," said Mrs. Conroy.

"We've noticed your restlessness," said Mr. Conroy. "What is on your mind, Evangeline? We'll support you as much as we can," continued Mr. Conroy.

"I have a huge favor to ask of both of you. I wonder- would you take care of Hope? I need to see if there's anything I can do to help end this war. It has caused me great loss. I don't want to chance losing my daughter, too."

"If that's what you feel you need to do, we would be honored to care for Hope. She fills our lives with so much joy. She fills the void of Liam being gone," said Mrs. Conroy.

"Oh, thank you both so much." She hugged and kissed both of them. "I love you so very much! I promise I'll find a way to visit often. I don't want Hope to not know who her mother is. I don't know how long this quest of mine is going to take. I hope for not very long. I want to get on with my life and live in peace. I don't think I can do that till I've made some things right. We both have relatives that are still fighting on opposite sides of the conflict. I want to help put an end to them killing each other."

Within an hour, Evangeline already having packed, she was on her way to the train station with Mr. Conroy. She was still crying from having to say goodbye to her daughter. She knew the Conroys would take good care of Hope. That was not the issue. She just wanted to be with her daughter. She and Mr. Conroy did not converse much. She knew he was feeling the anxiety of being separated that she was feeling. But she also knew that he would continue to be respectful of her wishes. She knew he wouldn't judge her in any way. She prayed on the way to the station that she would be able to see Hope soon. She prayed that she would return. She prayed the war would be over soon. She and Mr. Conroy arrived at the station, and they both stepped out of the carriage. They gave each other a hug, and she kissed him on the cheek. "I love you, dad."

"I love you too, Evangeline. We'll be praying for you." Then he turned, got back in the carriage, and left.

As Evangeline watched him drive away, her heart sunk. *Was she doing the right thing?* She hoped that she was, and turned toward the station office to get her ticket to Washington. She waited for her train for about an hour. It was late afternoon. She expected to be in Washington by nightfall. She was on her way to the War Department. On the train, she pulled out her Bible and read from Galatians. In verse 17 she read about Paul's going to Arabia and Damascus over a three-year period before going to Jerusalem after his conversion. He had needed time to prepare to be an Apostle. She felt she was on such a journey with God to determine what he would have her do.

When she arrived in Washington, she got a hotel room for the night. She settled into her room and soon fell asleep. She was physically and emotionally very tired. The next morning she would go to the War Department.

She woke early, washed, got dressed, and had some breakfast. She then took a carriage to the War Department. She was very surprised by all the women who were there. She had to wait a good while to talk to someone. Finally, a middle-aged woman called her over to her desk. "What's your name, young lady?"

"Evangeline Conroy, ma'am."

"What's your business?"

"I would like to know how I can serve the Union in the war."

"We're always in need of cooks and laundresses," said the woman.

"Is there some way I could work more directly in the war effort?"

"Would you consider being a nurse?"

"Are they all my choices?"

"Yes," said the woman.

"I'll consider all of those. Thank you, ma'am," replied Evangeline and turned and walked away. As she left the War Office, she was lost in thought. *Should she do any of those things?* She felt like she needed to make a deeper commitment. *What could that possibly be*, she thought. As she continued to walk, she was struck by an insane idea, but she felt like she must pursue it. She went to a nearby clothing store and bought some clothes that she knew she would need. Then she took a carriage back to her hotel. She changed quickly, cut her hair shorter, and headed back to the War Office to enlist. She remembered all the young boys she had seen enlisting before. She felt she could pass as one of them. When she arrived at the enlisting station, she was called forward by a gruff-looking sergeant. "Name."

"Ewell Conroy."

"Age."

"Nineteen, sir."

"You'll do. Go collect your uniform, rifle, and orders."

"Thank you, sir,' said Evangeline and picked up her uniform and gun. She found an empty closet, ducked into it, and quickly changed. She showed another sergeant her papers and was told where she should report. She did so and met some of the men she would be serving with. Then, since evening had come, she bunked down with the rest of the men for the night.

The next morning she was awoken by the sound of reveille. There was a quick breakfast and then training began. Evangeline was glad that it was cool, because her heavy blue uniform was very warm. The captain in charge of them began to drill them on battlefield maneuvers, explaining to all the recruits how important they were to staying alive during battle. As they were performing one of those maneuvers, Evangeline tripped on a stone and fell against the man next to her. They both fell down in the dust. "I'm so sorry."

"You stupid, kid," the man growled, laid both of his hands on her chest, and shoved her to the ground. As he did so, his eyes became very wide. "Captain, that boy is a girl, I think!"

The captain snapped, "Both of you, fall in over here!"

Evangeline and the man stood at attention before the captain. He walked up to Evangeline so that his face was right up to hers. "Are you a girl? Tell me the truth. Don't make me have to check."

Evangeline began to sob. "Yes, I'm a woman."

"What the hell are you trying to prove, missy? Women aren't allowed to fight in the army. Sergeant, take her back to the enlistment office. She must give up her rifle and uniform. Lady, you need to go home."

The sergeant took her back and she told them where she had stashed the clothes she had come in. They made her change, took her uniform and gun, and sent her out of the building. As she was leaving, she heard a voice behind her.

"I think I know a way you can serve your country. Are you interested?"

"Yes, I think so," said Evangeline. "Who are you?"

"I'm Captain Blalock."

"What would you have me do?"

"I have someone I want you to meet. What's your name?"

"Evangeline."

"Come with me, Evangeline. He'll explain to you how you can serve."

Captain Blalock led Evangeline upstairs and down a back hallway. He pushed open a door at the end of the hallway and motioned for her to go inside. Behind a desk sat a handsome, clean-shaven man.

"Hello, I'm Lafayette Baker. I recently became the Director of the Union Intelligence Service. I believe you're here because you want to serve your country. I can help you with that, if you're interested."

"Do you mean you're looking for spies? I don't think I could do that."

Captain Blalock spoke up. "Evangeline, you were going to fight on the front lines. That takes spunk. If you were considering that— "

"You can do what we're proposing," Baker chimed in. "The Union is in need of good women spies. Our best is a

Negro woman operating in South Carolina. We need more like her. The South has much more effective women spies. Two that we're watching closely are Belle Boyd and Antonia Ford. There was a third, Rose O'Neal Greenhow. She's gone to Europe to gain support for the Confederates we think. We think you might have what it takes. Would you be willing to join us?"

Evangeline thought for a few seconds. "Count me in. When do we start?"

8

STONEWALL FALLS

Within weeks Evangeline was working for the Union Intelligence Service. The Intelligence Service knew that the South had operatives in Washington, D.C., so they stationed Evangeline there in a popular hotel as a maid. Evangeline was very grateful for this, because she could go home frequently to visit her quickly growing daughter. She had already been able to single out one individual that looked suspicious and reported the information to Baker.

In those early months of 1863 Baker introduced her to Frankie Abel who was employed by the Intelligence Service to spy on Antonia Ford, a known Southern sympathizer and spy. Baker told Evangeline to particularly pay attention to any chatter about Antonia Ford. Then one day in March when she checked in with Baker, he jumped up from behind his desk, his face beaming. "We got her! She's been arrested. We are holding her at Old Capitol Prison."

Evangeline knew exactly who Baker was talking about. "Congratulations, sir. Let's hope that this gives us more of an advantage."

"It'll help, but the war's just dragging on. It's a significant drain on our resources. The only hope that we seem to have at present is that the Confederates have fewer resources than we do. Time should be on our side. But if this goes on too long, we may be able to win but not pull the Union back together." Then he gave Evangeline further instructions and sent her back into the field.

Evangeline continued to gather information over the next month or so and was able to identify other suspicious persons to watch in Washington. One morning in early May when Evangeline went to report to Baker, she once again found him to be very cheery. "You look very well today, sir," she said.

"Evangeline, I have very good news! I received a dispatch from one of our spies in the Confederate army. Stonewall Jackson was wounded days ago at the Battle of Chancellorsville and has died! That'll prove to be a major blow to the South. He was a great strategist and commander. Another spy we have attached to Lee's regiment has reported that Lee said the loss of Jackson is the loss of his right arm. Lee's said to be despondent. And the morale of the men is not good. The most interesting part about it is that Jackson was shot by his own army. They thought he was part of enemy troop movements."

"Oh, thank you, sir, for the information. Do you have any new orders for me?"

"No, Evangeline, just keep doing the fine work that you are. You've helped to uncover a couple of these sympathizers' plots."

Evangeline said goodbye to Baker and left his office. She felt that God had intervened and answered her prayers that the war would begin to favor the Union. She felt that the death of General Jackson was a sign of the providence of God. She felt that God wanted the Union to end slavery in America. She was elated! She didn't have to report to the hotel till the next afternoon. She decided to return to the

Conroy farm to visit her in-laws and daughter. The visit was good but much too short. She wondered how much longer she could keep going on like she was. It was taking a toll on her both physically and emotionally. She just wanted to restart her life with herself and her daughter. But the war wasn't going to allow that. She knew that she would have to continue what she was doing, because she was making a difference. To stop would be an abandonment of Liam's and her dream for their country.

In a couple of days, Evangeline returned to the War Department to check in with Baker as was customary. She knocked on the door and it took a few moments before someone opened it. It was Captain Blalock. She hadn't seen him for a couple of weeks. She noticed that he seemed to be distracted.

"Oh, Evangeline, come in."

"Hello, Captain Blalock. How've you been?" As she said this, she noticed that Baker quickly shuffled some papers into his top desk drawer.

"I've been fine, thank you," Blalock answered.

"Hi, Evangeline," Baker said, looking concerned but trying to hide it. "I've no one new for you to watch at present. Thank you again for being one of our best agents," he managed, trying to make conversation. "That'll be all. See you in a few days."

"Okay. See you then," said Evangeline and walked out of Baker's office. She was curious. *What was happening? Baker had always been very open to sharing important information with her. Maybe too open*, she thought. *What's this abrupt change?* She felt it must be really important. She had to know what was on the paper he had stuffed into his desk. She hoped it would still be there later, for she planned to find out. She needed to work at the hotel from late afternoon to early evening. When she was finished, she was going to break into Baker's office to read that paper.

Evangeline completed her shift and walked down some more remote streets to the War Department. Then she slipped into the alley behind the building and to a back door she knew well. It was always kept locked, so she had a key to open it. She put the key in the lock as she had so many times before and turned it. She went in and then up the back staircase to Baker's office. She paused for a moment before his door. She had come to the difficult part. She had to get Baker's door open. She took out the lock pick she had been given when she began spying. She had never had to use it. She hoped she could remember her training. She tried it once and couldn't get the lock to click. She tried it again and failed to unlock the door. She prayed that the Lord would help her. She manipulated the lock with the pick a third time. She heard it click, turned the knob, and opened the door. She went into Baker's office and quietly closed the door. She pulled out Baker's chair and attempted to open his top desk drawer. It was locked. She got out her lock pick and pushed into the lock. She maneuvered it in the lock and pulled on the drawer. It opened. She saw the paper she had seen earlier that day lying on top of a pile of papers. She pulled it out of the drawer and opened it up. She started to read it. It was more information about the death of General Jackson. It related how Jefferson Davis was furious about the major blunder of his own forces causing the death of one of his best generals. But the agent that had sent the dispatch said that Davis also appeared very alarmed. The agent stated that Davis' fear seemed to be generated by the presence of a man dressed in black, who remained in the shadows of the nearly dark room where he was meeting with Davis. The agent had no idea who this man was but related that he had a foreign accent. He felt that whoever the man was, he must hold a great deal of power to unnerve Jefferson Davis. The agent wondered if the South's "Cotton Diplomacy," its attempt to gain support from Britain and France by restricting trade on cotton, had backfired. The agent was unable to relate anymore information because he had been sent from the room. Evangeline folded the paper, put it back on the pile of papers in Baker's drawer, closed the drawer, and locked it. That mysterious paper had left her with more questions than answers.

She left Baker's office deeply puzzled. *Who was the man in black that seemed to frighten Jefferson Davis? What did Davis and the mysterious man discuss?* She intuitively knew Baker had the same thoughts. That was why he looked so concerned. He was fearful that Europe would side with the Confederacy. This also alarmed Evangeline. She began praying as she left the War Department building and walked back to her apartment. If Europe entered the war, the Union would have to fight a two-pronged war. She doubted that it could sustain that for very long. She had no idea what she could do under such circumstances. She asked God to show her what he wanted her to do next. She arrived at her apartment and tried to go to bed for it was quite late. She could not sleep. She stayed up and read her Bible. Eventually she drifted off to sleep...

She returned to Baker's office a few days later. He was obviously in better spirits. He greeted her warmly and said he had good news. "We arrested Belle Boyd and she's been banished to the South. If she's found anywhere in the North again, she'll probably be shot. It's great not to have to be concerned about her anymore. In fact, we need not be concerned with any of the three we've discussed before. Greenhow is in Britain."

"Why do you think she went to Britain, sir?" Evangeline wanted to probe to see how much Baker might reveal about European involvement in the war.

"Jeff Davis is trying to get financial support. The South's short on supplies. If the war keeps going on, I believe the South will collapse."

Evangeline pretended to be listening intently and to agree with him. She wasn't sure of his assessment however. The South seemed to be more than holding its own in the war. She felt that if they gained support from Europe, it would tip the balance in the Confederacy's favor. She realized the North desperately needed a major breakthrough. She prayed many times during the day that the Lord would bring one to the Union. She continued to fervently pray that night for a miracle. The North needed nothing less than a miracle of God.

9

GETTYSBURG

The miracle Evangeline had prayed for took place on July 1st-3rd, 1863 at Gettysburg, Pennsylvania. Lee had been successful at Chancellorsville. This encouraged him to attempt to invade the North a second time. This battle would cause the greatest number of casualties of the war for both sides. Its positive effect, however, was to once and for all put an end to Lee's push into Union territory in the Eastern Theater. Several actions caused this battle to be a miracle for the North. The first was the long absence of J.E.B. Stuart's cavalry during the crucial fighting of the battle. Secondly, Johnston Pettigrew grossly miscalculated the strength of Union forces in the Gettysburg area. The third was the failure of General Ewell to seize Cemetery Hill. Fourthly, Longstreet had not attacked as early and forcefully as Lee had expected. Fifth was the heroic action of Colonel Lawrence Chamberlain of the Union Army. His defense of Little Round Top during the battle helped seal the victory by the Northern Army.

Evangeline learned about the victory days after it happened when she once more checked in with Baker to report to him and receive any new orders. He was obviously in very good spirits because of the news, and Evangeline was elated. She thanked God for answering her prayer. "Sir, the victory is great news! The Union needed such a victory. The tide seems to be turning against the South with the loss of General Jackson and the capture of Belle Boyd."

"Evangeline, don't mention that name again."

"Sorry, sir, I won't." She wanted to ask him why but dared not to do so. "I'll leave, now, sir."

"Please call me Lafayette."

"Okay, sir—I mean Lafayette. I'll report back in a few days." She turned and left the office, feeling a little unnerved. That had been a very awkward encounter. She came to know why later. She learned that Baker had been accused of brutally interrogating Belle Boyd before she was released. Regardless of what she was later to learn, she already had become suspicious of her commander. She was believing more and more that she couldn't trust him. She made a mental note to herself to be very careful what she said and did around him.

She was beginning to feel that the North could win the war. She was also thinking that she might soon be able to give up the shadowy life she had been leading and return to a more normal one. She wanted so much to be with her daughter. She resolved at that moment to ask for a few days off at the hotel. Baker hadn't given her anyone new to keep a watch on. She believed he was thinking the war was well in hand. If she was going to see Hope, this was the time. She detoured toward the hotel, instead of going directly back to her apartment. She talked to the manager and was able to secure a few days off. She got on a train and headed home. From the train station she took a carriage and arrived at the Conroy's farm early in the evening. She knocked on the door and Mrs. Conroy answered it, holding Hope.

"Evangeline, it's so good to see you! We've missed you so much!"

Evangeline looked into her little girl's face and smiled. "Oh my, you have grown so big! I love you so much!' Then she took Hope in her arms and hugged her tightly. "Mom, I would like to sit on the porch alone with Hope for a while."

"Go right ahead, dear. I'm making dinner. Dad should be in soon from the barn."

Evangeline sat with Hope and rocked her. She was so grateful to be home again. She so longed that this would last and prayed that it would. She knew Liam would be so happy to have such a beautiful daughter. She hoped that he would be proud of what she was doing to help the Union achieve victory. She reveled in the moment. Soon Mrs. Conroy was calling her in for dinner. She put Hope, who had fallen asleep, in her crib. She washed up and greeted Mr. Conroy who was very happy to see her. They ate dinner, talked for a while, and then she went to bed.

She awoke the next morning to Hope's crying. She fed and changed Hope then decided to take a walk around the farm. The early morning sun was filtering through the trees, mingled with the mist that rose from the damp grass. She remembered being with Liam at such times. It brought tears to her eyes. She had so little time to think of him or to cry. She allowed herself the time to grieve. She felt a new sense of purpose. She knew she must continue her work till the end of the war. She couldn't allow Liam's death to be in vain. She prayed again that the war would end quickly so she could return to this farm. Then she put it all in God's hands. "Thy will be done."

After three full days of rest and being with her family, her daughter, and the Conroys who had become her mom and dad, she returned to Washington. Her first order of business would be to check in with Baker the next morning. She arrived at her apartment very late and went right to bed. She awoke early, changed, and had some breakfast.

Then she went immediately to Baker's office. She found him melancholy. "Where have you been? I expected you yesterday," he snapped.

"If you must know, I went home to see my daughter. You gave me no new persons to watch when I was here last, and the hotel gave me time off."

"Well, okay," he managed. "I've received more information about how the war is progressing. It's less than optimistic."

"I thought Gettysburg was a success," replied Evangeline.

"Maybe so, but it wasn't a crushing defeat. Meade could've brought a swift end to the war, but he was too cautious to pursue the Confederates. There are rumblings that President Lincoln is very upset. Apparently on July 4th, it rained heavily in the Gettysburg area and both armies decided not to engage in battle. Lee and his troops began to retreat. Meade and his forces followed slowly behind them. At the same time heavy rains had also flooded the Potomac and Lee was trapped for a while on its north side. His army would've been unable to escape, if Meade would've been more decisive. Lee's army crossed the Potomac before Meade arrived there. So the war will continue."

"I'm sorry to hear that, sir."

"I told you to call me Lafayette."

"I don't feel comfortable with that, sir," Evangeline respectfully replied.

"Have it your way!"

"Sir, do you have anyone new for me to watch? If not, I would like to get to work."

"Yes, I want you to keep your ears open about any men dressed in black that are staying in the city. My gut tells me I need to know who he is or they are. I believe there may be more than one."

"Alright, sir, I'll make that my priority. I'll let you know what I find."

"Thank you, Evangeline. You may go."

Evangeline turned and left his office, closing his door with a bang. She was upset. She didn't like the way Baker treated her when he was discouraged. She also was saddened by the news that the war maybe could have been ended, and the opportunity was allowed to slip away. Yet, she still believed a miracle of God had taken place. She felt that maybe it had been a miracle for both sides. Though Gettysburg probably drove the South out of Northern territory permanently, maybe God in His grace was giving the South another chance to not end up totally devastated. Maybe it would allow for brothers who had fought against each other to both save face. Maybe it would facilitate reconciliation for the nation and her families.

10

FATHER ABRAHAM

The situation with Baker improved slightly over the next couple of weeks. She had given him some solid leads concerning men dressed in black in the city of Washington. Unfortunately, though it seemed these persons surely existed, none of them could actually be located. Evangeline thought this would cause Baker to be more mean spirited once again. However, upon arriving at his office and meeting with him, he appeared to have taken on a demeanor of resolve. "Evangeline, I believe these shadowy characters dressed in black are here to determine what our overall war plan is. Thus, I'm expecting that their main efforts would be directed at this building and the White House. This building is already secured. However, I want more eyes in the White House. I'm going to transfer you there."

Evangeline was silent for a few moments. Then she replied, "That would be an honor, sir."

"You'll be going there in the guise of a housekeeper. You'll be going in there highly recommended by your current employer. You'll be working under Mary Ann Cuthbert, the Chief Housekeeper."

"When do I start, sir?"

"In a couple of days after I've made arrangements to have one of the girls in the White House dismissed."

"You mean I'll be taking away someone's livelihood? I don't—"

"Feel comfortable with that," broke in Baker. "It's for the good of your country."

"Will something be done for the person who loses her job?"

"I'll see what I can do, Evangeline. Now get yourself ready to move. I'll take care of what needs to be done about your apartment."

"Thank you, sir. I'll get on it immediately." Then she left his office and headed for her apartment. She walked as quickly as she could. She decided that she would get all of her belongings together hastily and then leave to go to the Conroy's farm, which she did. She spent a day and a half with her daughter and in-laws.

When she arrived back in Washington, she had to check herself. She had started to head for her apartment. Reality had not quite set in yet. She was going to live and work in the White House! She took a carriage from the train station near the Capitol Building to the White House. When she arrived there, she was greeted warmly by Mary Ann Cuthbert.

"Hello, Mrs. Conroy, I'm Mary Ann Cuthbert. I'm very pleased to meet you. You come highly recommended."

"Thank you. Is it all right if I call you Mary Ann?"

"Yes, of course. May I call you Evangeline?"

"Yes."

Mary Ann then showed Evangeline to her quarters and gave her a tour of the White House. She met several members of the staff as they went. But she had not yet seen the one she truly wanted to meet: Abraham Lincoln. She admired him so much, because of his perseverance in attempting to save the Union. "Mary Ann, will I get to meet President Lincoln?"

"Oh, yes, Evangeline. Mr. Lincoln is very interested in all of his staff here at the White House. At present he's not here. He's out fulfilling one of his many duties, I suppose."

"I'm so happy! I so want to meet him!"

"Let me take you back to your quarters, Evangeline. That completes our tour." They walked a little farther and then Mary Ann stopped in front of an open door. "Your room is here. Do you remember where my room is?"

"Yes, Mary Ann, I do."

"Meet me there tomorrow at eight. I'll go over your duties with you then."

"Thank you, Mary Ann. It's so nice to meet you."

"It has been nice to meet you, as well, Evangeline. See you in the morning."

"Yes, I'll see you then."

Mary Ann turned to go and Evangeline walked into her room and shut the door. This was really exciting for her. She couldn't believe she was in the White House. She unpacked her belongings, and since it was only late afternoon, she decided she would take a walk around Washington. The air was cool and crisp. She was invigorated by it. As she walked, she reflected on her life. It had been hard, having lost Liam. But it also had been much more interesting than she ever could have imagined. She sat down in the grass in a quiet place and began to pray. She prayed first for her little daughter and her in-laws. Then she began praying for her country. She admitted to herself that she was afraid of the future. She felt something secret and very sinister was going on behind all of the conflict of the war. She wondered if America would ever be the same. She sat there a little longer, lost in deep thought. Then she stood up and returned to the White House. By the time she arrived there, it was getting dark. She marveled at the rose-pink and deepening blue of the sky. This assured her that God was still in control. She did not need to fear for herself, her loved ones, or her nation. They were safely in God's hands. She entered the White House and went directly to her room. Once there, she washed up and went to bed. She fell asleep quickly and slept soundly through the night.

The next morning she arose early. She couldn't wait to get started! She knew that her job was important. She would help protect her President and nation. She was ready to do whatever she could. She would remain very alert.

She had some breakfast and went to Mary Ann's room. When she arrived, Mary Ann looked as though she was going over the schedule for the day. Evangeline knocked on the slightly open door.

"Come in, Evangeline. Are you ready to get started?"
"Yes."
"Let's get to it, then," said Mary Ann. Mary Ann then proceeded to show her where the linens were and trained her on how she should perform her duties. Then she left Evangeline alone to do her job and told her to report back to her when she had finished.

Evangeline worked quickly but paid attention to every detail. She wanted to make sure she would keep this job. When she had completed what Mary Ann had given her to do, she began to walk back to Mary Ann's room. On the way she spied President Lincoln with a bearded, bald man. She wondered who he was. She knew she must be suspicious of everyone around the President. She was going to find out who he was. She continued on to MaryAnn's room and checked in with her. Mary Ann assigned her to another room, gave her the same instructions as before, and told her that President Lincoln wished to meet her after her workday was complete. Evangeline couldn't wait! The rest of the day couldn't go fast enough.

President Lincoln met her near the Yellow Oval Room. At 6'4" he towered over Evangeline. He put out a large hand to greet her. "Hello, Mrs. Conroy. I'm very pleased to meet you. I'm happy that you have joined our staff."

"I'm so thrilled to meet you, Mr. President!"

"I understand that you are a widow. Let me extend my deepest sympathies to you."

"Yes, Mr. President," replied Evangeline, "my husband was killed at the Battle of Front Royal."

"To die so early in this horrible war... I'm so sorry."

"Thank you, Mr. President."

"I'm sure your husband was a good man. I hope you can forgive me."

"I don't hold you responsible, sir. My husband wanted to fight for what he believed in. And I was in agreement with him."

President Lincoln bowed his head and sighed. "So many lives lost."

"I believe God is on our side, sir. I believe we will win this war. I pray often that we will."

"I believe that, too, Evangeline. Will you pray for me?"

"Yes, sir, I will."

"Thank you, my dear girl. I so need it."

"You have my word, sir. I will pray every day."

"I would like to talk again some time, Evangeline."

"I would, too, sir."

"I'll arrange it for some time soon. You can catch me up on how your prayers are being answered. I must go now."

"I understand, sir. By the way, who was that man I saw you with earlier?"

"That was an old friend who I once represented when I was a lawyer."

With that they said goodbye to each other and Evangeline returned to her room. She had some dinner, read for a while, and then got ready for bed. She had been comforted about the man she saw with President Lincoln.

She still wondered who he was. She drifted off to sleep and dreamed about herself and Liam under their marriage tree. Peace would one day return to her life. One day all would be free . . .

11

FOUR SCORE...

The last couple of weeks had gone by quickly for Evangeline. She had been diligently watching for suspicious persons in the White House. She had not really uncovered anyone that she thought should be watched at that time. She hoped her lack of information would not stir up Baker's ire. Though she had little to report, she had come to realize that she did not care much for the Secretary of War. She did not trust him. She deliberated as to whether she should alert Baker about her feelings. She decided she would.

A few days later Evangeline met with Baker on a secluded part of the White House grounds. His presence was not questioned because he had met with both the President and Stanton at the White House previously.

"Well, Evangeline, have you discovered anyone of note who you think we should be watching?"

"No, sir, I have not."

"That is disappointing. So you have no information for me?"

"Not exactly, sir. But I don't trust Secretary of War Stanton. He always appears to me as if he's hiding something."

"Don't be concerned about him, Evangeline. He's solidly on our side." Then he shook his head and said, "Contact me if you uncover anything important." Then he walked away.

Evangeline was left standing alone and downcast. After a few minutes she returned to her quarters at the White House. She had some dinner and then took a walk around Washington. The cool night air helped her to clear her head.

The next day after she had finished her day's work, she met with the President again. He greeted her warmly.

"Hello, Evangeline. Have you been praying for me?"

"I have done so every day since we last talked, Mr. President."

He looked at her with melancholy eyes. "Evangeline, you seem like a bright young lady. I have many people giving me advice. In the end, however, I must make the decisions. I must do the hard things. I sometimes wonder if I have grown callous. In January of this year I called for the freedom of the slaves in this country. Having done that, I have unofficially made the freeing of slaves an objective of this war we are now engaged in. So the freedom of the slaves has been joined with our objective to save the Union. I wonder if I have made a mistake in doing so. There has been so much bloodshed. But I'm persuaded that the very freedom of our country is entwined with the freeing of the slaves. There are those outside this nation that would like to see us fail. What's your opinion?"

"Mr. President, I believe that if all men are not free, there truly is no freedom. I feel you are proceeding in the right direction."

"There's some movement in the legislature to introduce an amendment to the Constitution to abolish slavery in this country. I'm considering putting all my energy as the chief executive of this country to seeing it becomes a reality."

"I think that would be a good course of action, sir," answered Evangeline.

"Good. Will you pray for its success?"

"Yes, I will, Mr. President."

"I appreciate you very much, Evangeline. I and this country need all the prayers that can be sent up to the Almighty. We will not win this conflict without the aid of God."

"I agree," answered Evangeline. Then the President told her he needed to tend to some other matters of importance. As he turned to go, she asked, "When can we talk again?"

"I'll arrange for another meeting soon."

Much to Evangeline's dismay, they didn't meet for another few weeks. She felt the President was probably embroiled in the political wranglings that would be necessary to get the new amendment he'd spoken of introduced into the legislature. Finally when the day arrived for her to meet with him, she couldn't wait for her workday to come to an end. When she was summoned to see him, she was tempted to run but walked as fast as she could. She found him sitting in a rocking chair with his head bowed. She wasn't sure if he had fallen asleep from exhaustion due to all the stress he was under, or if he was praying. She tapped lightly on the slightly cracked door.

He looked up and said, "Come in, Evangeline. You probably thought I fell asleep. I was meditating on the words I've been asked to write."

"What words are those?" Evangeline asked.

"I've been asked to give a speech on November 19 when a national cemetery will be dedicated in Gettysburg. What a great task it is. How can mere words bring honor to what those brave men of the Union sacrificed on those three days? How can one show that the cause for which they gave their lives was a just one?"

"Sir, you are an honorable man. You're a man who seeks God's counsel. You'll find the words that must be said."

"I do hope that God will help me. I know you and others are praying for me and this nation. I believe He will answer for the sake of those prayers."

"I've found him always to be faithful, sir."

"Speaking of that, you have a daughter don't you?"

"Yes, Mr. President I do."

"How is she doing? I know you are making a great sacrifice not being with her every day. I cannot imagine not being able to be with Tad."

"I guess she's doing fine. My in-laws adore her and take good care of her."

"Evangeline, when did you last see her?"

"I went home a couple of months ago."

"I want you to take a couple of days and go see her. I'll arrange it with Mary Ann."

"Oh, Mr. President, thank you!"

"It's the least I could do for all those prayers you've said for me."

Evangeline thanked the President a couple more times and then left him. She had been so excited that she forgot to ask him when they would meet again. She hoped they would. At the moment, however, she was full of joy that she could go home to see her little Hope. She left the next day and returned to the farm. She spent two wonderful days loving her daughter and catching up with Mr. and Mrs. Conroy. Once again she didn't want to leave, but she knew she must return to Washington. There was still much work to be done.

The day she arrived back in Washington, she went to see Baker. He wasn't happy with her for taking days off, but he could do nothing about it since the President had given her the time. Further, he didn't want anyone in the White House to know that he had someone planted there. He thought the

President would be most furious with him. Evangeline left him, dismayed once more.

When she returned to the White House, she immediately began her work and watched for anything suspicious. Again, she didn't see anything that alarmed her. She did see the bald, bearded man, but wasn't alarmed since the President had called him his friend. She wondered what they talked about. In a few days she was sitting with the President once again.

"You know, Evangeline, I talk to my messenger, William Slade, daily. We talk about all sorts of things. I consider him my friend in the same way that I also consider you my friend. I've read some of the lines of the speech I told you about to Willie. I've done that a few times. I want you to hear the speech, too. But I want you to come to Gettysburg with my entourage. I believe you can be helpful to me there, and I'll have you praying nearby. That would give me great comfort. Edward Everett will be the main speaker. He's an excellent orator. Far better than I believe myself to be."

"Mr. President, I would be honored. Don't worry about him; just speak from your heart. I'll pray that God guides you."

Several days afterward Tad Lincoln became very ill and the President's wife became hysterical. She had already lost two young sons and was very distraught. The President thought he was going to have to cancel his trip, but assured Mrs. Lincoln that Tad would be alright. Mrs. Lincoln reluctantly allowed him to go. So on November 18 the President boarded a train for Gettysburg. Accompanying him was Secretary of State Seward, Interior Secretary Usher, John Hay, John Nicolay, a diplomatic corps, and others. He went under a military escort. Also with him was Evangeline Conroy.

This entourage arrived in Gettysburg later on the 18th. On the way to Gettysburg the President had told John Hay that he felt weak. His demeanor brightened when he was immediately handed a telegram that stated that Tad was doing much better. President Lincoln and those with him had dinner and were serenaded by the Fifth New York Artillery Band. After this, the President retired for the evening under close guard. Evangeline settled in for the night at the same time. She went to bed excitedly anticipating what President Lincoln would say. She couldn't sleep right away, so she prayed for him. She drifted off as she prayed . . .

The next day the ceremonies took place among the graves of the many that lost their lives during the Battle of Gettysburg. They commenced with music by the Birgfield's Band followed by Reverend T. H. Stockton who gave a prayer. There was more music by the Marine Band, followed by Edward Everett's oration which lasted two hours. A hymn written for the occasion was performed, and then it was time for Abraham Lincoln to speak. He rose and immediately began. "Four score and seven years ago..."

Evangeline was riveted on every word that the President spoke. She thought that he looked deathly pale. His speech only lasted a couple of minutes, and it was simple and straightforward. But Evangeline marveled at how it spoke to the condition of her country at that moment, the honoring of those who sacrificed their lives for the cause of the war, and the continuing work that had to be done for the nation to be preserved. After the President spoke, a dirge was sung, and a benediction was given by Reverend H. L. Baugher.

When the entourage boarded the 6:30 train for Washington, Evangeline overheard the President say that he was still feeling weak. He also stated that he was feverish and had a headache. Evangeline wondered what was wrong and wanted to go care for him, but she wasn't allowed near him. So she sat on her seat on the train and prayed for her President.

12

JOHN WILKES BOOTH

It had been three weeks since the entourage from Gettysburg had arrived back in Washington. In all of that time, Evangeline had been unable to see the President who was quarantined with a mild case of small pox.. It had become apparent when he returned that he had a more serious condition than what was originally thought. Not only did he continue to have the headaches and a fever, but he also developed back pain, exhaustion, and eventually broke out in a rash and sores. It was unclear as to how he had contracted the disease. Evangeline met with Baker the day following her arrival, and when she told him of the President's condition, he suspected that the President had been poisoned with arsenic. Evangeline wasn't sure why, and he was not forthcoming in telling her his reasons. It became apparent when the President broke out in a rash and sores that that was not the case. Her second meeting with Baker two days later was much less tense. Baker, being a little more relaxed, was more open with her. "I hope I didn't frighten you too much the other day. I'm becoming increasingly suspicious that forces outside this country want the Union to fail. It may be nothing more than some European countries fearing their economies may be disrupted. Or, there may be much more sinister activities being plotted. Either way I fear for the President's life. There are many, I believe, who don't want him re-elected."

"What more sinister things are you referring to, sir?" Evangeline asked.

"I'm not at liberty to discuss those, Evangeline. There's no proof, and I must keep the theories of certain people to myself."

"I understand, sir. Will there be anything more?"

"No, you may go, Evangeline."

Evangeline left his office and headed for the White House. When she arrived there, she immediately began her work. She was distracted, however, and found herself going over the same tasks. She knew she had to focus because there was a lot to be done, but she could not stop thinking about Baker's words. She was very concerned for her President. She wondered if the sinister forces that he referred to had anything to do with the men dressed in black. She was determined that she was going to find out. She decided that she was going to double her efforts to find out about them. She prayed that God would help her to do so. She felt that since she hadn't seen any of them in the White House, she would have to go out into the city and look for them. She made up her mind that she would begin that very night after she was finished work.

As soon as Evangeline had finished work and had some dinner, she left the White House and began walking the streets of Washington. She walked for a couple of hours in close proximity to the White House and discovered nothing of import as she watched all activity carefully and listened to the conversations of other streetwalkers. Then she returned to the White House and readied herself for bed. She couldn't go to sleep and lay there with her mind racing. She was upset that she had found out nothing. She finally settled on a plan.

The next night she determined that she would take a carriage to another part of the city and walk it. Then she drifted off to sleep.

The next morning she was up early, had some breakfast, and commenced her work immediately. She was much more focused and accomplished all of her duties and attended to some extra tasks that had been identified if all other work had been completed. As she was finishing, Mary Ann approached her.

"Hi, Evangeline, how are you doing?"

"Hello, Mary Ann. I'm doing well."

"I'm glad to hear it. I just wanted to tell you again that you're doing a great job. I'm very pleased with your work. However, I noticed yesterday that you seemed to be distracted. Is everything alright?"

"Yes, I'm fine."

"I know you haven't seen your daughter for a while. As soon as I can, I'll let you take a couple of days off to see her. Unfortunately, things are hectic here because of the President's preparations for re-election, and this illness has complicated things more."

Evangeline asked, "How is the President?"

"He is doing much better. He should be fully back to work in a couple of days," replied Mary Ann.

"That's good to hear."

"Yes it is. I'll let you go."

"Thank you, Mary Ann. You've been really good to me. I appreciate it so much."

Mary Ann continued down the hall and Evangeline hurried back to her quarters. She changed quickly and headed out into the streets. She hired a carriage and rode for about a mile. "You can stop here, driver."

The driver stopped the carriage and she got out. Then she began walking the streets as she'd done the night before.

After a while she arrived in front of Ford's Theater. There was an old billboard there for a play that had starred John Wilkes Booth. She'd heard that the Booth family was one which boasted of three talented actors: Julius Brutus Booth, the father, and John and his brother Edwin. She thought it might be a good idea to go to a play. She never really allowed any time for pleasure in her life. She continued walking until she had to stop in order to get a carriage back to the White House. Once again she'd discovered nothing about the men dressed in black. She wondered, as she sat in the carriage, who these men were that they could hide so easily. By the time she'd made it back to the White House, it was once again time for bed.

She awoke very early the next morning because she needed to check in with Baker. She was to meet him at their usual place on the White House grounds. As she approached him, she could tell that he was agitated. He was pacing back and forth and seemed to be talking to himself as though rehearsing a speech.

"Good morning, sir."

"Why are you always so cheery? Do you not understand the gravity of the situation?"

Evangeline was almost afraid to ask. "What situation are you referring to, sir?"

"I am speaking of President Lincoln's re-election of course. A lot of people don't want him back in office. It's so bad that the Republican Party is hard pressed to come up with a strategy to assure his re-election, and President Lincoln is our only hope to save the Union. The armies of the North have made little progress in defeating the Southern forces and there have been many casualties. People are growing tired with the war effort. If President Lincoln is not re-elected, I fear there'll be a movement to abandon the cause of saving the Union. There needs to be a strong show of authority by the Union, not just for that reason but also because Napoleon the third has placed Archduke Maximilian as the Emperor of Mexico. That's a direct violation of the Monroe Doctrine. We cannot allow Europe to interfere on this continent."

Evangeline acted as if she knew nothing of what Baker was talking about. "I don't really understand what that all means, sir."

"It means that it's absolutely essential that President Lincoln is re-elected next November. I can't really do anything about him being re-elected, but I'm going to make sure to the best of my ability that nothing happens to him. Do you understand that?"

Once again Evangeline felt she was being rebuked by Baker. "Yes, sir, I understand what you're saying. How would you like me to proceed to accomplish that end?"

"I need you or someone to find out more about these men dressed in black. Can you somehow double your efforts to get me some solid information on them?"

Evangeline answered, "I've already begun to do that, sir. I've been walking around town after my duties at the White House are complete."

Baker was visibly impressed, and his attitude toward her softened. "That's very good work! I knew you would be good at this when I chose you. I should've known you would be on top of the situation. Please carry on, Evangeline. I'll be waiting for what you can dig up."

"Thank you, sir. I'll keep at it. I'll be in touch." With that she walked away, grinning with satisfaction. She felt like this had been her first real victory over Baker. Her hard work and perseverance had finally paid off. She walked into the White House and immediately set about doing her job. When she had completed her duties, she again went out into the city in search of information. She continued to do this night after night for over a week without discovering anything of consequence about the men dressed in black. She was becoming really frustrated and remembered that she'd promised herself a night at a play. It was Thursday. She decided the next night she would go to Ford's Theater.

Before she knew it, her Friday was coming to a close and she had completed her workday. She went to her quarters to change, had some dinner, and got a carriage to the theater. She arrived there half an hour before the play was to start. As she was entering the theater, she saw a face she recognized. It was John Wilkes Booth! She thought it was strange that he was there because he wasn't acting in the current play. She thought about walking over to meet him, but she decided not to. As she was heading to her seat, she heard Booth bragging about himself to another man that appeared to be an actor. She stopped for a few seconds and caught part of the conversation before she continued to make her way toward her seat. As she did so, she heard a voice behind her.

"Hello, miss, I noticed you walking by just now. I hope you don't mind me telling you how lovely you are."

Evangeline turned red and became flustered. "Oh, thank you, Mr. Booth."

"So you know who I am."

"Yes, I do."

"Well, what's your name?"

"I'm Evangeline Conroy."

"I'm going to still be here after the play. Could I buy you a drink? Could we talk then?"

"Mr. Booth, I'm married and I don't drink."

"I'm sorry. You're not wearing a wedding band."

"That's because my husband was killed in the war but I have a child."

"I'm so sorry, Evangeline. Forgive me for taking up your time."

"That's quite alright, Mr. Booth." With that she turned and walked to her seat in the theater. She thought that had been a very strange encounter. She still wondered why he was present at Ford's theater. She shrugged it off, sat down, and immensely enjoyed the play.

The next day after she had completed her work at the White House she was delighted to hear that President Lincoln had asked for her. She walked quickly to where she had been directed she would find him. She found him standing by a window, reading. She tapped on the slightly opened door.

"Come in, Evangeline. I've missed meeting with you. I hope all is well."

"Yes, Mr. President, I'm doing fine. I've missed you, too. How are you doing?"

"Well, considering all that has transpired. How is that daughter of yours?"

"I have not seen her for a while."

"What am I going to do with you, Evangeline? You must go home and see her."

"I'm going to in a couple of days, sir. Mary Ann has already given me time off."

"Good. Good. I presume you've been praying for me and the nation?"

"Yes, sir. I have."

"Thank you, my dear young lady. I feel you're going to pray this war to victory."

"I hope so, sir. I have a question. Do you know John Wilkes Booth?"

"No, I don't personally know him. I've seen him act, however."

"Can you tell me what you think of him, Mr. President?"

"He pointed his finger at me three times during the play, 'The Marble Heart.' I thought that a bit unusual. I have no thoughts about him otherwise. Why?"

"I just wondered. I met him last night. I felt very uncomfortable around him," she answered. They talked a little longer, and she got up from the chair she was sitting in and began to go.

"Pray I get elected, Evangeline," he said as she left him.

13

RE-ELECTION

*E*vangeline's routine of working as a housekeeper and spy in the White House by day and combing the streets of Washington by night had dragged on for weeks. The only respite she had had was to visit Hope and the Conroys for a few days around Christmas. She was frustrated that she had not been able to uncover any valuable information about the men dressed in black. She had also grown very weary of Baker. She never knew what to expect when she met with him. She longed for the war to be over, so that she could go home permanently. She had contemplated telling Baker she was done. She could not bring herself to follow through with doing it, though. She knew she had to complete what she'd started. She needed to honor her husband's sacrifice and to try to reconcile her family with the Conroy family. She hadn't seen President Lincoln since before Christmas. That also added to her melancholy. She understood that the President had many issues with which to contend, and that he was very busy. She just missed their talks so much. She prayed she would be able to see him soon.

A few days later, her prayers were answered. President Lincoln called for her while she was still working. This really concerned her because she was afraid she would lose her job. Mary Ann had come to get her, and though she said nothing, she looked very annoyed. Evangeline was sure that something must be wrong for the President to do such a thing. As she walked toward the Yellow Oval Room, she prayed that she would be up to whatever situation in which she found herself, that the meeting would not keep her from her work for too long, and that she would be able to complete her work for the day.

When she reached the Yellow Oval Room, she found President Lincoln shuffling through a stack of papers. He appeared to be unfocused and disorganized. She walked into the open doorway. "Hello, Mr. President." She tried to sound cheerful.

"Come in, Evangeline. I must be brief for both our sakes. I hope there are no repercussions with Mary Ann. Please tell me if there are. I need you to pray very specifically for me."

"How would you like me to pray, sir?"

"I am contending with three major issues. The first and foremost is the passage of the Thirteenth Amendment. In case I'm not re-elected, I want to ensure that all men are free as you've so aptly put it. It will once and for all abolish slavery in our nation. I believe that it will pass in the Senate without too much difficulty, but I still feel the need to monitor it closely. The House of Representatives I believe will present us with a much different matter. Getting it passed there will consume a great deal of my time, I fear. The second issue is who I should put in charge of the Union armies. General Meade's performance has been less than exemplary. I'm very disappointed with his performance since Gettysburg. The last issue is dependent, I believe, on the success of the others. My re-election is dependent on the Union war effort improving, and I'm sure that the passage of the Thirteenth

Amendment will help to strengthen and pull together the Union government leaders. I really need you to pray fervently for these things. I've witnessed that your prayers are effective."

"Mr. President, I will gladly pray for you in all of that. Is there anything else that I can do?"

"No, Evangeline, I'll let you go."

The President looked back down at the papers on his lap and began shuffling through them once again. Evangeline left quietly. She headed straight for the room she had been working on. When she arrived there, the room had been completed. There was a note on the bed. Evangeline unfolded it and read it. It was from Mary Ann. She wanted Evangeline to come to her room immediately. Evangeline was very fearful. She expected that she was about to lose her job. As she walked toward Mary Ann's office, she prayed for the Lord's favor.

Mary Ann was waiting for her when she arrived. She was visibly upset. Evangeline prepared for the worst.

"Evangeline, you've been a very good worker. I've appreciated it and have rewarded you for your good work. I don't understand all of these visits with the President, but it's really not any of my business. That is, it's not my business when they take place on your time. What has happened today, however, is another matter. I will not allow your visits with the President to disrupt the work schedule. The President has already apologized to me for the inconvenience. I'll let that be sufficient. I want you to know, however, that I've told him there can be no more meetings during your work hours. Now please go back to work."

"Thank you so much, Mary Ann," said Evangeline and quickly left Mary Ann's presence. She thanked God for His mercy. She was sure it would not go well with Baker if she got fired. She was so glad that she would not have to tell him about the incident. She felt very beaten up and exhausted.

She hoped she would be able to get through the rest of her workday. She doubted she would be doing any reconnaissance in the streets of Washington that evening.

She worked feverishly, pushing herself beyond what she thought she could bear. When she finished her last assignment, she trudged her body to her room. She lay down on her bed and fell asleep immediately. She dreamed she was tied to a chair, and that the gruff voice of a man was shouting at her from somewhere in the darkness of the room where she was being held. She pulled with all the might of her arms, attempting to loosen the ropes around them. As she did so the man came closer. She did not recognize him, but something about him seemed familiar . . .

She awoke in a sweat. She couldn't retrieve an adequate picture of the man in her mind. She was now wide awake. She knew she wouldn't be able to sleep for a while. She decided she should go back out onto the streets of Washington. She got out of her sweaty clothes and left the White House. The air was cold but felt really good on Evangeline's face. It was welcomed after a day of disappointment and fear. She sat down on a bench and looked up at the stars. There were many, for it was a clear night. She thought back to all the nights she and Liam had laid in the grass and watched the stars overhead. She began to cry. She didn't know how much longer she could sustain the double life she was living. It had taken a toll on her that she couldn't have imagined. She took a couple of deep breaths. She sighed and looked up at the heavens once more. Liam was out there somewhere. His quest for justice and her continuing love for him would give her all that she would need to continue on. She got up and walked back to the White House. It was later than she'd thought. She settled back into her room and sat down to read. She fell asleep in the chair.

For the next couple of days, she concentrated only on her housekeeping work. It paid off because Mary Ann softened toward her. She had once again become her congenial self. Evangeline was very relieved because she was due to meet with Baker once again. The meeting didn't go well. Baker was upset that she'd discovered nothing new about the men in black. He was particularly upset that she'd stopped going out on Washington's streets at night.

"Why have you stopped looking for those men, Evangeline?"

"I 've been very tired, sir."

"I know it's a strain, but we must determine if the President is safe."

This triggered a thought in Evangeline's mind. "Sir, maybe I do have something to report. When I was talking with the President, he informed me of an incident that occurred last fall. The President went to see the play, 'The Marble Heart' at Ford's Theater. John Wilkes Booth was the star of the play. The President told me that Mr. Booth pointed at him three times. The President thought that was strange. I don't know if it means anything."

"It sounds like you are grasping for straws. Find out about those men in black!"

Baker walked away, shaking his head. Evangeline stood there sobbing for a few minutes. Then she wiped her tears away and proceeded to the White House and work.

Before her next scheduled meeting with Baker, he sent her a note not to contact him again until she had some pertinent information to share. He told her he was too busy to spend time on her trivialities. Thus, Evangeline had no contact with him for almost two months. In that time, the future of the Union looked like it was becoming brighter. The President had named a new commander of his army: Ulysses S. Grant. He had taken Vicksburg the previous year which had given the Union control of the Mississippi River. President Lincoln and other Union leaders were very confident in his leadership and ability to win the war. Also the Thirteenth Amendment vote had just passed in the Senate on April 8th. Half the battle of its ratification was complete. Time would prove, however, that it would not pass so easily in the House of Representatives.

As that political conflict began raging in the nation's Capital, a series of bloody and lengthy battles began to be fought in Virginia. They were all part of Ulysses S. Grant's "Overland Campaign." The first of these was the Battle of the Wilderness which took place on May 5-7, 1864. Part of the Battle of Chancellorsville had been fought there the previous year. There were over 25,000 casualties. The majority of these were suffered by the Union. Immediately following the Battle of the Wilderness, Grant once again engaged Lee's forces in the Battle of Spotsylvania. This battle cost the Union another 18,000 men. Lee's forces lost 12,000 men. Ten days after Spotsylvania, the Battle of Cold Harbor was fought. The first two battles did not yield any clear-cut victor. Cold Harbor, however, was a Confederate victory. The Union once again had lopsided casualties. They lost another 13,000 soldiers to the South's 2,500. Grant's army, though, kept pushing up against Lee's forces. Three days after the Battle of Cold Harbor ceased, General Meade crossed the James River and engaged General Beauregard's troops of the Army of Northern Virginia at Petersburg. The Union losses were over 8,000 men, again far more than the Confederate's 3,200. The North's Army of the Potomac lost the conflict which set up a long and bitter siege of the city of Petersburg. The bad news of the losses of battles and life slowly trickled back to Washington, and Evangeline learned of them from Baker. Once again, she found herself near despair as she realized that the war effort would be prolonged by each Union defeat. She began to pray every chance that she got in addition to her morning and evening prayers.

Further adding to that burden, things were not going well for the North in Washington either. President Lincoln's re-election campaign was not off to a good start. The Republicans had to create a new party, the National Union Party, to attract enough War Democrats and Border State Unionists to give the President a fighting chance at re-election. This brought about a compromise that gave the nomination for Vice President to War Democrat Andrew Johnson. And the President was forced to personally lobby State Representatives to attempt to get the Thirteenth Amendment passed in the House of Representatives. When Evangeline was finally able to quickly meet with the President once again, she found him haggard and cursory.

"Evangeline, I don't have much time. I'm sorry our meeting must be brief. I have missed talking with you. I just wanted to thank you for praying for all those things we've previously discussed. Please continue to pray. Things are not going well on any of those fronts. Some people are concerned for my life. They need not be. I must take the risk. If I don't get elected, I fear we might not have a Thirteenth Amendment or a Union."

14

SURRENDER

A few weeks later the Battle of Monocacy had taken place and the Confederacy had gained still another victory. That victory brought the armies of the South to just outside of Washington. As Evangeline considered that, she felt that God had done another miracle for the North. The Confederate Army had won the battle, but the Union's General Wallace had slowed the advance of General Early. He had given Early's forces enough resistance to exhaust them. Instead of attacking, Early retreated.

Washington, D.C. had been spared! Evangeline thanked God for his intervention.

A couple more months slowly passed, and Evangeline kept asking God to help her overcome the drudgery she was feeling. She had rarely gotten to see Hope or the Conroys. Meeting with Baker was always a challenge. Trying to uncover the men in black was a constant frustration. The highlight of her life had become being a housekeeper. She wondered if that was just the way it was going to be during the remainder of the war, or if God was preparing her, like Moses in the desert all those years, for something greater.

She wasn't sure, but she continued to fight the temptation to become complacent.

Then after several difficult meetings with Baker, she hoped her first meeting with him in October would be an improvement. She left the White House quite early in the morning to prepare herself for another of Baker's sour moods. The air was chilly, and she could see her breath as she exhaled. A light mist hung in the air. She waited for him and tried to keep herself warm. He finally approached her. He had a smile on his face, something she had not seen for a long time.

"Evangeline, I have great news! Rose O'Neal Greenhow is dead!"

Evangeline thought it odd with all that had been transpiring in recent months that Baker would focus on the death of a woman, even if she was a spy. "Oh, wonderful, sir," she managed. "When did that happen?"

"Just days ago when she attempted to stealthily re-enter the country. She was returning from Europe. Jeff Davis had sent her to England and France to try to gain support from them for the Confederacy. I've been told that she met with both Queen Victoria and Napoleon III. She was aboard the British blockade runner, *Condor*, which was stopped by our navy. She apparently tried to escape in a rowboat which capsized, and she drowned. Her body was just found yesterday, according to the report I recently received. I was also told that she was returning with gold to help the Confederate cause. It won't help them now."

Evangeline listened with mixed emotions. She was overjoyed that the gold that Greenhow was bringing to the Confederacy had been seized, but she was saddened by Baker's gloating over the death of the woman. And suddenly she understood Paul's words that our enemy is not flesh and blood, but the wicked powers of darkness that prevail upon people to do evil. She didn't answer immediately, attempting to find something to say. "Well, sir, I'm glad the gold didn't get into the South's possession."

"Is that all you can say? Sometimes I wonder whose side you're on. I have to remember you are a Marylander."

"What is that supposed to mean?" asked Evangeline. "Do you doubt my loyalties?"

Baker was taken back by her response. "Well, no."

"I'm glad to hear it. Will there be anything else?"

"No, you can return to your work."

Evangeline, both frustrated and angry, left him with disgust. She prayed that the Lord would forgive her attitude as she entered the White House. She decided she would be the best housekeeper she could be for that day and each one after, until the accursed war was over. She completed her duties, had some dinner, and went immediately to bed. The streets had no draw for her that night. She awoke the next morning and began her routine all over again. This went on for another month.

Then like a bright star on the horizon, Abraham Lincoln was re-elected President of the United States. Evangeline was relieved and couldn't wait to meet with him again. They had met very little since he had begun to seek re-election.

She met with him a few days later and noticed that he seemed less burdened. For the first time, she met him on the White House grounds. It was warm for that time of year. He was standing, looking off into the distance.

"Hello, Mr. President."

"Good morning, Evangeline. How are you doing today?"

She wanted to share her frustration but knew she couldn't. She had to keep it bottled up inside. That was the hard part. She was thankful she knew God and could pray. "I'm doing alright, Mr. President. You're looking much better."

"I am? I'm glad to hear it. I need to exude a sense of confidence if we are to prevail in our endeavor to win the war and the freedom of the slaves."

"Well, sir, you've completed step one. You'll be President for four more years. You've won a great victory."

"No, my dear Evangeline, we've won a great victory. You and many others like you who have prayed and believed. I'm grateful, but our work isn't done. The Thirteenth Amendment still needs to pass in the House. Can you find it in your heart to continue to pray? I know the burden of it grows with each day."

"With God's help I can, sir."

"Good. I'll arrange for us to meet regularly again."

"Thank you, sir. I'll look forward to those meetings as always." Then she said goodbye to President Lincoln and left to commence her workday.

Christmas came and went quickly. Evangeline was able to spend a few days with Hope and the Conroys. She cried all the way back to Washington, wishing she had not had to leave. Yet she was encouraged because she felt God was telling her that soon the war would be over. *What a joyous day that would be,* she thought. She closed her eyes and envisioned what it would be like to spend every day with her daughter and in-laws. She felt at peace for the first time in a long while.

Evangeline continued her routine through the remainder of December and into the month of January. She was thankful that she had her housekeeping job to keep her busy. Gathering information on the men dressed in black continued to bear little fruit. The good news was that there had been little fighting through the early part of the winter. It seemed both armies had pretty much encamped for the cold weather. At least a temporary end had come to the great number of casualties on both sides. Evangeline gratefully thanked the Lord for that. And she was elated when circumstances started to begin to favor the North once more. First of all, she learned that the Union's blockades of supplies and weaponry to the South had begun to be very successful. The Confederacy was beginning to suffer severe shortages of food and supplies particularly. Many of their soldiers were starving and had deserted. Secondly, on the last day of January the Thirteenth Amendment passed in the house. All of the nation's slaves were one step closer to realizing their freedom. Evangeline began to feel that both of President Lincoln's great objectives— freeing the slaves and saving the Union, would soon be obtained. She couldn't wait to meet with him again to congratulate him. She did so a week later. She found that he was much more relaxed and himself. He was also much more optimistic about the Union's war effort. That was short-lived, however. When she saw him again in late February, he was once again more concerned about bringing as quick an end to the war as possible. She found him hunched over in a chair, staring at the floor.

"Good afternoon, sir."

"Is it afternoon already? Come in Evangeline. I seem to have lost track of time. I've been lost in thought, I must confess."

"Is there anything wrong, Mr. President?"

"Actually, Evangeline there is. I fear I had a chance to end this war, and I let it slip through my fingers."

"What do you mean, sir?"

"There had been a peace conference planned between Confederate delegates and myself and Secretary Seward. It might have been the last chance for reconciliation between the North and South. Jefferson Davis wanted me to recognize the independence of the Southern states as part of the peace negotiations. I refused. I'm wondering now if I made a terrible mistake."

Evangeline was disappointed and her face showed it.

"I can see that you feel I've done the wrong thing."

"I don't know if it was wrong or not, sir. I'm sure you have a much better understanding of the current state of affairs than I do. I'm just disappointed. I've been so longing for this war to end, so I can go home."

"Evangeline, do you need your job here? If not, maybe it's time for you to go home. I've appreciated your service here, and I've greatly coveted your prayers. They've given me the strength to continue on in the great endeavor in which I and this country have been engaged. You've been so selfless, giving up much of your time that could've been spent with your child. Maybe you just need now to be a mother."

"I'm honored by your words, Mr. President, but I made a vow that I would see this through to the end. I need to do so to honor my fallen husband's name. Otherwise, I'm afraid that he will have died in vain. I cannot let that happen."

"I understand, Evangeline. You remind me of my own words in my speech at Gettysburg."

"Your speech really inspired me, sir."

"And your prayers have inspired me, young lady. I have to go. I trust, though, that we'll see each other again."

"Yes, Mr. President, you can count on it," Evangeline replied. Then they both left together. She headed for her quarters, and he walked the opposite way. After taking several steps she turned around and saw the President with the bearded, bald man that she couldn't identify. She wished she knew what they talked about. Then she resumed making her way to her room. It had become dark outside. She had some dinner and returned to the streets of Washington. As she walked against the cold night air, she prayed that it would all be over soon. Walking the streets brought no reward. The war was stealing her life away. After a while, she began to shiver. She entered a nearby hotel and sat down in the lobby. Nearby was the bar. There were many people talking, but she still recognized one of the voices whispering not far from where she sat. It was Baker! She was determined to find out what he was saying. She walked a few steps closer and slipped into a chair with its back facing where the two men were. She strained to hear what Baker was saying. The first voice she heard was one she did not recognize.

"Mr. Baker, I tell you I have spoken with the President and with the Secretary of War. They both acknowledge the threat, but they aren't taking it seriously, I fear."

"Mr. Morse, what then can I possibly do about the situation?"

"You can take what I say and at least check it out. I tell you the President is in danger from this foreign threat. You wanted to know who these men are. I have told you. You are an investigator. Go find the proof you need."

"Mr. Morse, I've had people on this for months."

"Mr. Baker, that's because you're not looking for them in the right places. They blend in very well. They have been practiced at it for a long time. Go study a history of Europe. If you look deeply enough, you'll discover their similar intrigues there. They are well-versed in deception, fomenting discord, and murder."

"You don't leave me with much, Mr. Morse, but I'll follow up on what you've told me."

"Please do, and let me know if you find out anything significant."

"I'll do that, Mr. Morse. Good evening."

"Good evening to you, Mr. Baker, and thank you for the drink."

Both men rose and walked right past Evangeline. She was very relieved when they both walked out of sight. She got up and took a carriage back to the White House. She went over in her mind all of what she had heard as she rode back. She was determined to find out who Mr. Morse was. She got ready for bed but could not sleep. After a long time she drifted off and dreamed again about the man with the gruff voice. This time he never appeared. She awoke and wished she could remember what had seemed familiar about him the first time.

As soon as she woke, she had to get up because she remembered she had to meet with Baker. She was exhausted, but she managed to dress quickly and go to her usual meeting place on the White House grounds. Baker was there waiting for her.

"Have you any information for me, Evangeline? I need to know quickly. I have to go out of town for a while."

"I'm sorry, sir, I don't have anything new to report." She expected this would make him angry once more, but he listened and said nothing at first.

"You know, I've come to believe that finding the men in black is really of little import. I think we're chasing after shadows. I'm not so sure we need you at the White House any longer. I could probably make better use of you elsewhere. I'll let you know of my decision when I return. I see no further need for you to go out into the streets of Washington at night any longer. Just keep your eyes and ears open at the White House."

"Okay, sir, may I go to work? I don't want to be late."

"Yes, you may go."

With that they parted. Evangeline was disappointed. She wanted to remain close to the President. She prayed that the Lord would arrange for that to happen somehow. But she would not see Baker for many weeks. In the meantime she discovered that Mr. Morse was Samuel F. B. Morse, the painter and inventor of the telegraph. She thought his involvement in all of this to be odd. She hoped to learn the connection. During this time, President Lincoln also gave his second inaugural speech. A little over a month after the President's inauguration, General Lee evacuated Richmond. Soon followed the Battle of Appomattox Court House, and the Confederate forces, finding themselves surrounded, surrendered to Ulysses Grant and his army on the same day. The war between the North and South was unofficially over, though some fighting continued on into the month of May.

When Evangeline heard of the surrender, she was ecstatic. She started to plan her return home in her mind. She could not wait to be with her daughter every day. She determined that she only needed to tend to some formalities with Baker to finish out her career as a spy. She was so looking forward to being a regular citizen again.

15

SIC SEMPER TYRANNIS

It had been two days since Lee had surrendered at Appomattox. Evangeline had not met with Baker. In fact, she was not even sure if he was in Washington. She had already begun to pack, though she had to continue to carry out her housekeeping duties.

Her desire was to give Mary Ann her resignation, but she was still in the employ of Baker and did not want to prematurely end her assignment. She felt she needed to remain his spy in the White House till he gave her the word that her mission had been completed. However, she was starting to feel like nothing more than a maid because the pace of activity at the White House had waned considerably. It seemed as though everyone was much more relaxed than at any other time since she had arrived. Even the President looked much less haggard. She so wanted to meet with him to congratulate him. She wanted to say goodbye to him and wish him the best in his second term. But the President had not sent for her, so she waited hopefully.

Evangeline worked her day, changed, and had some dinner. Evening had come, and she considered what she might do to pass the time until she retired for the night. She decided to take a walk around the White House grounds. It was early April and the air was cool, but it felt like spring. Evangeline felt that it was God's way of telling America that all would be well. She hoped that the nation would experience a rebirth, as nature was again coming to life after the barrenness of winter. As she was finishing her walk and returning to her quarters, she was surprised to see that a large crowd had gathered outside the White House. Their desire was to see their President. They were calling for him to appear. There was a celebratory mood among the people. Evangeline had the feeling that they wanted to thank President Lincoln for accomplishing what had eluded the country for four long years. The dream of once again being a unified country seemed to be at hand.

Shortly the President appeared and stood at the window over the White House's main entrance. Though he didn't appear as burdened as he had for much of the war, the President was obviously deeply pondering what he was about to say. A man stood beside him with a light, so the President could read his notes. Tad Lincoln was also standing by his father. President Lincoln spoke about how the Southern states were improperly aligned with the Union and his plan for bringing them back into a proper position. He outlined how the process needed to be a gentle and not a harsh one. He spoke of how freed Negroes were to be a central part of rebuilding the state governments of the South. As he finished his speech and people were beginning to leave, Evangeline saw John Wilkes Booth in the crowd. He appeared angry, and so Evangeline turned away from him in the hope that he hadn't seen her. Unfortunately he had and walked over to her.

"Hello, Miss Evangeline. It's nice to see you again."

Evangeline turned around slowly to face him. She noticed that he did not appear angry anymore. "Hello, Mr. Booth," she replied. She was perturbed that he had called her "miss," but decided she would say nothing about it. They exchanged some small talk between them, and then he pressed her for her opinion of the speech.

"Well, Miss Evangeline, what did you think of the President's remarks?"

Evangeline hesitated and then answered, "I don't know much about these things, but it sounds like a good plan."

"So, you think it will work then?" he asked.

"I only hope it does, Mr. Booth."

"Well don't get your hopes up too high. It looks to me like a lot of people here were not expecting such a stance. I believe the days ahead will be bitter for the South. I'm convinced that it will not work, and I don't think it will happen. In fact, I'm sure of it!"

The way Booth talked made Evangeline shudder. She wanted to get away from him as soon as possible. He made her feel very uncomfortable, just as he had the last time they'd met. "I must go now, Mr. Booth."

"I wish you would call me John."

"I don't feel that is appropriate, Mr. Booth. I hardly know you."

"Well I do hope you have a good rest of the evening."

"I bid you the same, Mr. Booth," she said and walked away toward the White House. Never looking back, she entered the White House and went directly to her room. As soon as she got inside it, she locked her door. She didn't care how famous a man he was. She thought he was creepy. Her body shivered at the thought of him. She changed into her bed clothes, washed up, and went to bed.

Three days passed and it was Good Friday. She was planning to go to church that afternoon as she always had. She also had determined to go to the play, "Our American Cousin" that night. She had so enjoyed the theater when she went the first time that she decided she would go once more before she left Washington. She worked in the early morning and then went to church, having gotten the rest of the day off to do so. After church, she returned to her quarters, dressed up for an evening out, and got something to eat. Then she hired a carriage and made her way to the theater. The weather had become foggy. She felt the play would be a great remedy for the dreariness of the night. On her way there, she prayed that she would not run into John Wilkes Booth again. She prayed that if he was there, the Lord would conceal her presence from Booth.

When she arrived at Ford's Theater, it was already overflowing with people. She surmised from the large crowd that was in attendance that it would be a good play. The play began, and she was thankful that she'd not seen Booth anywhere. At about 8:30 the play stopped. Evangeline looked around to determine the reason for the delay. Then she saw President Lincoln, his wife, and others enter the box where he would be seated. The orchestra immediately began playing "Hail to the Chief," and everyone stood up and clapped. The President and the others in his box sat down, and the play resumed. The theater had a chill about it that Evangeline couldn't explain. She wrapped herself more tightly in her shawl. She also noticed that the President had gotten up to put his coat back on.

When the time for the intermission came, Evangeline got out of her seat to walk around a little. She was tempted to go up to the President's box to greet him, but she decided that would not be proper. Besides, she believed the President was due some time to relax and spend time with his wife. She really wanted to see him once more before she left Washington for home. She returned to her seat, and shortly afterward the play resumed.

At one point in the third act, actor Harry Hawk's lines brought a loud clamor of laughter from the audience. The laughter abruptly stopped, however, as a figure dropped to the stage yelling, "*Sic semper tyrannis!*" It was John Wilkes Booth. He ran away limping. As he moved out of sight, people in the theater began to panic. Evangeline looked around and noticed that frantic activity was taking place in the President's box. Mrs. Lincoln was screaming. Someone called out for a doctor. Evangeline's blood ran cold and her body quivered. She knew that something terrible had happened to the President. She wanted to do something, but she felt powerless to do so.

Under the direction of a Doctor Leale, some men were carrying the President's body out of the theater. They took him across the street to a house. Evangeline stood outside the house with the other people that had gathered there. Several doctors made their way into and out of the house. When questioned about the President's condition, they would only remark that it was grave. Evangeline couldn't believe what had happened and was in shock. She waited outside all night for a word about President Lincoln. It finally came at about 7:30 the next morning. It was announced that the President had passed away. Up to that time Evangeline had kept her emotions in check. With the word of the President's death, however, she began to sob and weep uncontrollably. It seemed as though almost everyone she'd ever loved had been taken away from her as a result of the war.

As Evangeline slowly composed herself, her thought was that she needed to locate Baker. It had been many weeks since she had met with him. She hired the first carriage she could and headed to the War Department. When she arrived there, she ran upstairs to Baker's office. His door was locked. Her mind was racing. She forced herself to calm down. Then she thought of Captain Blalock. She decided that her best course of action was to find him. As she walked down to the main level of the War Department, she wondered why

Baker had been absent for so long. It was a curious thing and very unlike him. As much as she often disdained his attitude toward her, she couldn't accuse him of being derelict to his duty.

When she reached the main floor, she looked around for someone to ask about Captain Blalock. The War Department was curiously quiet. She guessed that the news of the President's death had been discovered, and that the search for his assassin was being fully carried out. She realized she was not going to get any answers there. She decided to return to the White House.

When she arrived at the White House, there was a flurry of activity as preparations were being made for Vice President Johnson to take over as President. She was stopped at the entrance and asked what her reason was for being at the White House. She told them she was a housekeeper there, and Mary Ann verified that. Once in the White House, she went first to her quarters. Then she began walking the halls, and memories of her talks with President Lincoln came back to her. She stopped and began to cry. As she was sobbing, she heard a voice she recognized.

"Evangeline, I must talk to you."

She knew it was Blalock. She looked up and ran over to him. She threw her arms around him and held on to him. Slowly he put his arms around her.

"Captain Blalock, it's so good to see you. What's happening?"

"That's what I must talk to you about, Evangeline. Much has happened since I last saw you."

"Where's Director Baker?"

"That's a long story. He's in New York. He was demoted by Stanton and sent there."

"Why, Captain?" asked Evangeline.

"He suspected Stanton of corrupt actions and had tapped the Secretary's telegraph lines. Stanton sent the Director away and effectively shut us down."

"Well, who's going after John Wilkes Booth then?"

"From what I have been able to learn, Stanton has recalled the Director. He's on his way back to Washington. I wanted to know if we can count on you if we should need your assistance."

Evangeline hesitated. She wanted so much to go home and end this nightmare that she'd been living. "Yes, Captain, you can depend on me. The President was my friend. I want to see his murderer be brought to justice."

16

FALLEN COLD AND DEAD

Evangeline tried to busy herself with her housekeeping duties. It was a few days before she actually met with Baker. Upon his arrival in Washington, Baker had sprung into action immediately, sending dispatches to his operatives in a large area around the city. He had not wanted to meet as a group because he didn't trust Stanton. Blalock had contacted her the previous day and told her that Baker would meet with her at the hotel where she'd previously worked. She waited for him for over half an hour. When he sat down across from her, he looked excited. He greeted her warmly.

"Hello, Evangeline. It's been quite a while. I hope you're doing well. It's nice to be back in Washington again. I want you to know that we've made four arrests, and I have obtained the names of two more conspirators. This was a well-planned plot. I had hoped that we would have captured Booth by now, but he's still on the loose."

"It's nice to see you, sir." Evangeline couldn't believe she'd said it, but she really meant it. As much as she had had difficulties with him, things seemed safer with him around. She felt he was in control of the situation. She actually was disturbed that her feelings about Stanton seemed to be true. She wondered how anyone could feel secure if there were doubts about the dealings of the Secretary of War. "I'm sorry you were sent away, sir. I'm sure the situation is very difficult for you."

"Thank you, Evangeline, but I'm the one who is very sorry for not listening to you and your feelings about Stanton. I was blindsided because I didn't heed your words. Please forgive me."

"I do forgive you, sir. Now how can I help you?"

"I want you to infiltrate Stanton's office. I want to keep a close eye on him. I need someone there, and you're one of my few agents that he doesn't know. Are you willing to do this?"

"Yes, sir, I am, but what about my job? I mean my cover at the White House?"

"I'll take care of that. Just get ready to start there tomorrow."

"Okay, sir, I'll be ready."

Early the next morning Evangeline found herself in the War Office in Secretary Stanton's office. She was sitting, waiting to be briefed as to what her duties would be. After about 15 minutes, the Secretary himself came out to greet her.

"Good morning, Mrs. Conroy. It's a pleasure to meet you." He held out his hand to shake hers. "Haven't I seen you somewhere before?"

"I don't believe so, Mr. Secretary. It's nice to meet you as well," Evangeline managed. She actually didn't care for him at all, as she'd expressed to Baker before. She knew, however, that she had to make him believe that she did. The success of her mission demanded it. "I'm anxious to get started."

"Follow me. I'll show you to your desk. There is much to be done. We want to be faithful to President Lincoln's policies for rebuilding the Union. I believe the military will play an important part in that. There will be much administration. That's where I hope you'll be of great help. I've been told by an important person who knows of your work that you'll be most helpful."

"I certainly hope that will be true, sir."

"Well, here is your desk, Mrs. Conroy. I'll have someone over shortly to get you started."

"Thank you, Mr. Secretary."

With that Stanton turned and walked back to his office. Evangeline was so happy that her encounter with him had come to an end. She didn't know why, but she just did not trust the man. She waited for about 10 minutes when a bespectacled, thin man came up to her desk.

"Hello, young lady, I'm Mr. Watt. Let me acquaint you with the work you'll be doing here at the War Office."

Evangeline wanted to greet him in return, but he immediately began to show her what was expected of her. He spent about 20 minutes with her, pointed her back to where her desk was, and told her to come to him with any questions. She had none because she had helped her father with similar paperwork on the farm. She worked her day and then walked to the apartment that Baker had provided for her nearby. She was so glad to be out of the War Department. She just didn't like the atmosphere there. It had been one thing to meet with Baker there for short periods, but it was quite another to work there all day. She got herself some dinner and got ready for bed. She was exhausted. She believed it was because she'd been so nervous all day long. She hoped that Stanton would not be able to figure out that he'd seen her at the White House.

The next day she was up very early to meet with Baker. She'd thought that the meeting time was too soon, but he'd insisted. She really was afraid that he was going to be unpleasant with her again because she'd not discovered any useful information. The sun had barely come up when he walked up to her.

"Hello, Evangeline, I don't have much time. I'm still making last-minute arrangements for Mr. Lincoln's return to Illinois. I'm thankful that Blalock will be there. I know I can trust him. He has been faithful for many years. He's a good man. There aren't too many people that I trust in this city. Have you any information for me?"

"No, sir, I'm afraid I don't. They kept me very busy with a backlog of paper work. I promise I'll be diligent."

"I know you will. I also trust you. I have to go now. I'll want to meet with you in about five days or so. That should give you some time to dig up something."

"I'll do my best, sir."

"I believe you will, Evangeline. Good luck."

Baker then briskly walked away. Evangeline also walked quickly to the War Office. She didn't want to be late. She went straight to her desk and set to work. She worked quickly but accurately all morning long. Then she took her lunch break. As she was returning to her job, she heard the whistle of the 12:30 train. She knew that her beloved Mr. Lincoln was on his way home. She began to weep quietly. She wanted so much for her nightmare to end. She only wanted to be a mother to her daughter whom she hadn't seen for quite some time. She prayed for the Lord's strength. That gave her the resolve to return to work.

Evangeline spent the next several days doing her job and keeping as close an eye as she could on Secretary Stanton. She felt a new sense of purpose. For the first time in a long while, she actually wanted to please Baker. She knew it had been difficult for a man like him to apologize. So when she met with him a few days later it was with a renewed sense of purpose. As he approached her, she noticed that he walked with an air of triumph in his step. He quickly closed the gap between himself and her.

"Good morning, Evangeline. How are you doing on this fine day?"

"I'm doing better, sir."

"Good, good. I'm glad to hear it. What has Secretary Stanton been up to these last days?"

"He's been busying himself with details about maintaining the martial law that he has imposed on Washington, sir."

"Do you sense anything suspicious in his actions, Evangeline?"

"No, sir, I don't. He seems to be doing his job and doing it well. I'm wondering if I misjudged him before?"

"You're having second thoughts about him?"

"Yes, sir, I am. He appears to be missing President Lincoln. He seems genuine in his desire for justice to be done."

"Well, I had you come earlier than usual because I have much to relate to you about our ongoing investigation and apprehension of Booth. I first want to tell you that my men caught up with Booth and an accomplice near Port Royal, Virginia. The man with Booth— David Herold, surrendered. Booth wouldn't give up and was shot. He's dead."

Evangeline was caught off guard. She was surprised that her reaction was a sinking feeling in her stomach. All she could think of was that another needless death had occurred. She didn't like Booth. She would have expected her reaction to be one of satisfaction. "So we'll never know the why of what he did."

"No, Evangeline, I'm afraid we won't."

Evangeline wasn't sure, but she felt as though Baker wasn't being completely open with her. She waited for him to continue.

"The interesting thing about Herold, whom we've questioned, is that he somehow knew which road to take out of Washington that would allow Booth to escape. The other interesting thing is that there was an escape route at all, considering that Stanton had declared martial law."

Evangeline felt as though Baker was trying very hard to cause her to feel that the Secretary of War hadn't been above board in his actions. Again, she waited for him to continue, not commenting on what Baker was revealing.

"My men in various areas around the Capital have, further, rounded up seven other conspirators."

Evangeline was taken back by this. Not only was she surprised by the number of people that Baker was saying were involved, but she was wondering how Baker was able to track down so many persons in such a short time.

Baker paused for a moment and then continued, listing out the other suspects that had been captured. "We also have captured George Atzerodt who was to have murdered Vice President Johnson, and Lewis Powell who attacked and badly injured Secretary Seward, his son, and a bodyguard. These were the worst offenders, but we also took into custody Mary Surratt who owns the boarding house where the conspirators met, Michael O'Laughlen, Samuel Arnold who was part of Booth's original kidnap plot, Dr. Samuel Mudd who knew Booth previously and set his broken leg the night of the assassination, and Edmund Spangler who made arrangements at Ford's Theater which facilitated Booth's murder of President Lincoln. We're still looking for Mary Surratt's son, John, who was Booth's primary co-conspirator and a Confederate spy. He wasn't seen by any of our witnesses in Washington that night, but I believe he was here. I think he would have wanted to be nearby for the completion of his and Booth's plan."

"Well, sir," Evangeline replied, "I congratulate you on rounding up Mr. Lincoln's murderers so quickly. I guess this will give Secretary Stanton a renewed belief in your abilities." Evangeline could tell that Baker was trying to hide a smile.

"I hadn't thought of that, Evangeline. I guess you're right. Well, I must be going. There will be a lot of interrogations of the prisoners. Continue to keep an eye on Stanton. I'm still concerned about that road that he left unguarded. I'll arrange to meet with you in a few days."

"Okay, sir, I'll see you then."

Baker walked, as he had approached, quickly away. Evangeline stood and watched as he disappeared. She wasn't sure what she should feel. She was glad that all those involved in Lincoln's death had been caught, but an uneasiness about her boss sent shivers through her body. She made up her mind that she would be closely watching him as well as Stanton.

Evangeline didn't meet with Baker after a few days because President Johnson had ordered that the conspirators appear before a commission of nine military leaders. And within a week the commission had convened. Evangeline figured that Baker was probably holding, or taking, a prominent place at the proceedings. She also noticed the lack of Stanton's presence at the War Office. She wanted so much to know what was going on in that courtroom. She decided she would try to track down Captain Blalock. She thought he might be willing to reveal to her how the proceedings were going. He'd always been kind to her. She felt it was the least she deserved for all the sacrifices she'd made to help the Union war effort.

Evangeline finished her work for the day and hung around the War Office for a while, hoping she would see Blalock. He didn't come to the War Office that day, but she vowed she wouldn't give up. Her persistence paid off and she saw him entering the building the next morning. She followed him in and waited till he walked down an empty hallway before calling out to him softly, "Captain Blalock."

He turned around quickly, surprised that someone was behind him.

"Evangeline, it's nice to see you. How are you doing?"

"I'm well. I hope you are the same."

"Yes, I am. Thank you."

"Can I speak with you briefly, Captain?"

"Of course you can. You've earned it."

"Thank you, Captain. I was wondering if you could tell me how the proceedings are progressing."

"I wouldn't share this with just anyone, but, again, I think you've earned it. The prisoners have all been read the charges against them. The commission will start to hear testimony in a day or two."

"I guess Secretary Stanton and Director Baker are right in the middle of it all."

"I believe so, but I'm not privy to all that's happening, Evangeline."

"Why is it all so secretive?"

"I'm really not sure. I know there are congressmen, cabinet members, and others who are questioning why this is going to be a military trial. There has even been talk that it's unconstitutional."

"What do you think, Captain?"

"I'm concerned that it's happening too quickly. I want the President's murderers to be brought to justice, but not at the expense of people's rights. Don't tell anyone that I told you this, but I've heard that some of the prisoners are being kept hooded."

This caused Evangeline to shudder. "Who ordered that?"

"I'm not sure."

"Was it the Director? I have heard that his interrogation techniques are brutal."

"I really don't know, but I suspect it might be him, Evangeline."

Evangeline wanted to tell Blalock her suspicions, but all she had was notions. Besides, she wasn't sure if she trusted Blalock enough to express them to him. She decided she needed to meet with him more to fathom where he stood. "Can we meet again, Captain?"

"Yes. But you have to promise me you'll call me Ben."

Evangeline felt uncomfortable about calling him by his first name, but she decided that she needed to do it. She wanted to be able to keep meeting with him. "Okay, I promise I'll call you Ben."

"I'll get word to you when we can meet again."

"Thank you, Ben." She was surprised at how easy that was to say.

"You're welcome, Evangeline," he replied and turned to go.

She watched him walk out of sight, and then proceeded to the office where she worked. She had a hard time concentrating all through the day. She couldn't wait to meet with him again. She felt there might be some underhanded dealings in the investigation and trial, and she suspected that Baker and Stanton might be involved. If that was so, she wanted to expose them. She, at the very least, wanted to discover what all the secrecy was about.

Over most of the next two months, Evangeline and Captain Blalock met several times. He passed on to her in great detail all that transpired in the courtroom. He made it clear to her from the beginning that the position of the defendants was very serious. He related how the conspirators could be convicted by a simple majority of five, and that the death penalty could be imposed by a two-thirds vote of six.

He also explained to her that the defendants were in a most precarious position because not only were they on trial but the trial was being used to vicariously convict Booth, Jefferson Davis, and the Confederate Secret Service. As the weeks progressed, evidence was submitted that the Confederate Congress had appropriated five million dollars toward a plan and the implementation of subversion against the Union. It was uncovered that this operation had been active for most of the war. It was also cited that this operation had been run out of Canada. It was also learned that John Surratt, the conspirator who got away, had escaped into Canada. Further, it was shown that the South had even planned and used diseases such as yellow fever and smallpox against the North, particularly targeting President Lincoln and Union troops.

As Evangeline listened, she wondered if that was how President Lincoln had contracted smallpox around the time he delivered the Gettysburg Address. She was truly taken back by the breadth of the conspiracy. She wondered if the men in black she'd so long pursued had come from Canada. Unfortunately, she was left with more questions than answers.

As Blalock continued to relate the progress of the hearing, Evangeline could clearly see that the evidence was mounting against the Confederacy and its attempt to rid itself of Abraham Lincoln and other Union leaders. For the conspirators themselves, the evidence seemed ironclad for some and very circumstantial for others. Powell had obviously attacked Seward, his son, and bodyguard. Herold had been captured helping Booth escape. Arnold had most assuredly participated in the earlier plot to kidnap the President. O'Laughlen also had been proven to be involved in the assassination plot. As for Atzerodt, a revolver, a knife, a map of Virginia, and a bank book belonging to John Wilkes Booth had been found in his Washington hotel room. The most conclusive evidence against Mary Surratt was that conspirators had met at her boarding house for five to six weeks before the assassination. Also two carbines and ammunition had been stored at her boarding house for a time before the assassination. The only evidence against Spangler was that he'd asked someone to hold Booth's horse and had had a conversation with Booth about helping the assassin. As for Doctor Mudd, several witnesses testified that they had seen Mudd and Booth together several times in Maryland. It was also testified that he'd been at Mary Surratt's boarding house in March about a month before the assassination.

By June 29, the military commission rested from any further testimony and met in secret to consider all of the evidence. At the end of their deliberations they passed down four prison sentences and four sentences of execution on the conspirators. Spangler was given six years in prison. Arnold, Mudd, and O'Laughlen were given life sentences. Atzerodt, Herold, Powell, and Mary Surratt were sentenced to be hanged. They were executed on July 7.

Evangeline didn't go to witness the hangings. She was thankful that her beloved President's death had been avenged, but she was uneasy about how justice had been meted out. The thought foremost in her mind was that the war was officially over, and yet it continued to cost more lives. She wondered if the North and South could ever live in peace again. She felt that bringing the former Confederate states back into the Union was going to be an arduous and lengthy endeavor. She prayed that God would give the Union's leaders great compassion and wisdom in handling such a monumental task.

17

CARPETBAGGERS AND SCALAWAGS

After the executions, the government began to return to a new normalcy under Andrew Johnson. There was a general feeling in the land that justice had been served. However, there were some who were not completely satisfied. Certainly Evangeline had doubts about all that had transpired. Though she strongly desired to return home, she felt compelled to continue working at the War Office. She felt that Baker and Stanton had both acted suspiciously. If they were hiding something, she wanted to know what it was. And it began to become clearer in her first meeting after the execution. It happened a few days afterward when she was contacted surprisingly by Blalock. She was unsure as to why the change had taken place, and Ben, as she had become accustomed to calling him, thought it equally unexplainable. The one thing she was sure of was that Ben Blalock was a much gentler person. He always helped her to feel at ease. She, for the first time, really focused on the man that approached her. She realized that he was a handsome, well-built man. She suddenly felt something that she hadn't felt in a long time. She buried it deep inside herself.

"Hello, Evangeline, thank you for meeting me on such short notice. Director Baker sent me to relate to you that he believes you have fully completed your service to the Union Intelligence Service. He told me to tell you that the war is over, and that he believes there is no further need for you to spy on Stanton. In fact, he and Stanton are working together to try to capture John Surratt. They both believe that that is glaring unfinished business, as far as the Lincoln assassination is concerned."

Evangeline was stunned. She probably shouldn't have been. She knew that this time would come. But it was the fact that she felt a sense of betrayal that really surprised her. She knew she would not be able to let it go, for she had been drawn too far into the web of intrigue. Going home at this juncture would leave too many unanswered questions. She deeply longed to be able to spend many years raising her daughter, but not at the expense of letting truth slip away. She knew she was going to have to disclose to Ben what she was thinking. She carefully considered her words, then began: "Ben, I'm not sure that is the wisest course of action."

"What do you mean, Evangeline? I thought you wanted to return home to your daughter. He's releasing you to do that."

"I do very much want to be with Hope, but I have concerns about all that has transpired."

"What are your concerns?"

"Well, you know that the Director has had me keeping a close watch on Secretary Stanton since the Director returned from New York. He told me then that he didn't trust the Secretary of War. He even apologized to me for not listening when I told him that I didn't trust Stanton. Now you're telling me that they are working together to capture Surratt. Doesn't that seem strange to you?"

"Maybe the Director has had a change of heart. After all, Secretary Stanton seems to have done all that is humanly possible to continue what President Lincoln had been working to accomplish."

"Maybe he has, Ben, but there are still the allegations of the Director's brutality with prisoners. And I can tell you that he's treated me gruffly often. As for Stanton, why was one road, the one Booth escaped on, left unguarded during his imposition of martial law?"

"Those are good thoughts, Evangeline, for which I have no answers. And as we are now talking, I'm feeling that I need to tell you about how the Director secured that position. It was immediately after the debacle of Antietam in 1862. President Lincoln removed McClellan and when he did, then Director Allen Pinkerton was removed with him. My understanding is that Pinkerton was a very capable investigator, and there has been some questioning as to why he was also removed. He has since started his own detective agency. Anyway, when the office of Director was vacated, Stanton hired Lafayette to take over. So it does seem very interesting that they have such a distrust for each other."

"Maybe they know each other too well," replied Evangeline.

"What do you mean?"

"Maybe theirs is an unholy alliance based on mutual distrust because each one knows what the other is capable of."

"In other words, Evangeline, you think they may have been working together on some secret plan?"

"I certainly believe that's possible."

"Evangeline, I believe it's your and my duty to keep an eye on the Director and the Secretary. If there has been some sort of foul play devised by them, I feel we must be responsible to expose it."

"I agree, Ben. How are we going to make that work?"

"I'll keep a close watch on the Director. I still work closely with him."

"What about me? How can I help?"

"We need to find a way to keep you close to the Secretary. Now that the war is officially over, there's little need for you in your current capacity. Besides, the Director's a shrewd man. He'll become suspicious, I believe, if we place you too close to the Secretary. Also, he'll wonder why you aren't going home to your daughter. He's well aware of your desire to do so. And I believe you need to be with Hope. She needs her mother full-time."

Evangeline was struck by how much Ben sounded like President Lincoln. He, too, had expressed the same thought. And deep within her heart, she knew they were right. Ben had a sensitivity that few men she had encountered in Washington possessed.

She again felt a stirring within that she hadn't felt for a long time. This time she decided she needed to pay closer attention to it.

Ben continued, "The Director trusts me. If I make a recommendation, I believe he'll act on it. And I think that the Union's plan for reconstruction of the Southern states may open up a possibility to keep you close to Secretary Stanton. The military will be playing an important role in that plan for at least the beginning of it. Given some of the hostile sentiments that many in the North are harboring, I believe some oversight of the military's actions in the South will be needed. I'll suggest to the Director to recommend to Stanton that former Union agents should be used because they have proven that they can be trusted. I'll also suggest that you be one of them."

"But that still doesn't address my desire to be with my daughter. I feel the Director will be suspicious."

"We are going to remove any suspicion, Evangeline, by bringing Hope here to live with you."

"You could make that happen, Ben?"

"Yes, I think the department can facilitate that."

"Who will take care of Hope, though, while I work?"

"How old is Hope now? Is she three?"

"Yes, she is three."

"Would you feel comfortable taking her with you? I feel that would actually be an advantage for what I'm considering. A mother and daughter would appear very non-threatening."

"What are your thoughts, Ben?"

"I believe we could set you up to make trips to Southern states to observe the military's actions there. Then you would return to Washington to report what you've witnessed. That could give you ongoing access to Stanton, even if it's indirectly. What do you think? Would you be willing to do it?"

"I am. Keep me posted. In the meantime I'm going to go home."

"Good, Evangeline. Enjoy your daughter. I'll be in touch."

"Thank you, Ben," replied Evangeline and she hugged him.

He slowly put his arms around her and then held on tightly to her. Then he let go, smiled, and said, "I'm looking forward to seeing you soon." Then he began walking away and turned to look back at her once more.

Evangeline watched him fade from sight, and then she prepared to go home to her daughter and in-laws. It had been a long time since her last visit. She left the next day and was able to stay a few weeks. The affect of it was to revive her body and soul. When she was finally contacted by Ben, she was ready to return to Washington. But this return was so much sweeter because Hope was going with her. She tearfully said goodbye to Mr. and Mrs. Conroy and told them she would stay in touch with them and promised that one day she would return for good.

After arriving back in Washington, she began her new assignment within a couple of days. She was first sent to Tennessee. She wasn't sure why. She had thought she would probably go first to Virginia. Though she questioned it, she followed her orders and observed the army's handling of the situation there. After doing so, she reported back to the War Department what she had seen. As it turned out, Tennessee became the first Southern state to be re-admitted to the Union the following year.

Her routine quickly became one of traveling to a state, observing the army's actions, reporting to the War Office, noting Stanton's activity as much as was possible, and meeting with Ben to pass on what she'd discovered. This went on for months. As the year progressed, two major developments took place. The first was that the presence of Union troops in the South sparked frequent unrest and protests, some violent. The other was that the North's troop strength steadily dropped from about a million in May to only 152,000 by the end of 1865. The lesser number of troops didn't bring increased peace, however.

All during this time, Evangeline realized that a very important occurrence had also taken place in her life. She was falling in love with Ben Blalock. She began to wonder if he was experiencing similar feelings. During their next meeting, she felt compelled to determine if he did. When he walked up to her, she quickly took him by the hand and looked into his eyes, not saying a word. He returned her gaze and pulled her close to himself. Then he bent down and kissed her on the lips. She felt a surge go through her body that she thought she'd lost. After they'd kissed, she said, "I love you, Ben."

"I love you, too, my beautiful Evangeline."

They were together as much as possible as 1866 commenced. They were married in May, and she moved to his residence immediately afterward. During that time the road to reconstruction continued to be a rocky one. Also, Baker and Stanton closely worked together to capture and bring to custody John Surratt. He was finally arrested by American officials in Egypt in November of 1866. He was returned by boat to the United States and arrived at the Washington Navy Yard in early 1867.

After his capture he was interrogated extensively. As Baker learned new information, he would discuss it with Ben Blalock whom he continued to trust without reservation. He didn't suspect that Ben was conversing with his wife. Thus, during the time preceding Surratt's trial, Evangeline and Ben learned some very interesting facts about what Surratt had been doing since the assassination. They discovered that from Canada he had fled to Liverpool. He stayed there briefly and then traveled to Italy where he served in the Zouaves, the Pope's elite guard, under the name John Watson. Both Evangeline and Ben found that to be a very interesting piece of information. They thought that even considering that Surratt was a Roman Catholic, how did he make such an unlikely connection? They further learned that he'd been recognized, arrested, and sent to Velletri Prison from which he somehow escaped. Again, they were suspicious. When he escaped, he'd somehow made his way to Egypt. That, too, intrigued them.

Surratt's trial commenced soon after his return to America. He was tried in a civilian court. The only charge for which the statute of limitations had not passed was murder. The prosecution wasn't able to prove that Surratt had anything to do with President Lincoln's murder. A mistrial was called and he was released .

Evangeline and Ben were disappointed. They felt that Surratt had somehow escaped justice. And their suspicions were again raised when information was released that Stanton wouldn't at first hand over John Wilkes Booth's diary, which was in his possession. When he finally did hand it over to authorities, it was discovered that the diary was missing 18 pages. Stanton couldn't adequately explain why the pages were missing. They also learned that Stanton had received the diary from Baker and a Colonel Everton Conger. He'd taken it off of Booth upon his death under orders from Baker. Thus, they continued to spy on Baker and Stanton, and they witnessed that both of those men were incensed at Surratt's release. Evangeline and Ben felt that the anger displayed by the Director and the Secretary went deeper than a miscarriage of justice.

As 1867 continued to unfold, Evangeline and Ben watched as President Johnson fired Secretary of War Stanton who refused to leave office. President Johnson then declared that Stanton was dismissed. Baker then inexplicably came to Stanton's defense, accusing the President of corruption. President Johnson reacted by accusing Baker of spying on the White House and firing him. This then led to nine charges of impeachment against President Johnson, seven of which involved removing Stanton from office. Both Evangeline and Ben suspected that Stanton and maybe Baker were behind the movement to impeach the President. Their suspicions were further fueled by Baker's perjuring himself during the impeachment proceedings. As it turned out, President Johnson was acquitted of the charges against him by one vote shy of the two-thirds needed to convict him.

Evangeline and Ben continued to search for the evidence that they suspected existed which would bring Stanton and Baker to justice. It never came. But as though God demanded that justice be done, as Evangeline was later to express to

Ben, both men died shortly thereafter. Baker's death on July 3, 1868, was supposedly from meningitis. There were some who conjectured that he'd been poisoned. Stanton died on December 24, 1869, officially of respiratory failure four days after being nominated to the Supreme Court by Ulysses Grant. Rumors spread that he'd committed suicide.

Evangeline and Ben decided to end their quest. They felt they could accomplish no more. The Civil War was over, America seemed to be on the road to reunifying as a nation, and all of the essential players of a real or imagined scandal had been forgotten or had died.

EPILOGUE

General Grant became the 18th President in March of 1869. The stormy Presidency of Andrew Johnson was over. There were high hopes that the celebrated General would be able to make more progress in unifying the nation than what had transpired to that time. Unfortunately, President Grant's administration was mired by many scandals due to his appointment of corrupt individuals. This caused the attention of the people to be distracted from the importance of reconstructing the South. Adding to that distraction, the nation also suffered from its first industrial age depression and the ensuing mad scramble to get out from under hard times. By 1877, at the conclusion of his second term, Grant left office with the knowledge that most of the progress he'd made had been undone.

Evangeline and Ben had been given land by the Conroys and had built a modest house on the farm. Ben had retired from the military and sold his residence. He was receiving a pension and helped Mr. Conroy, who was finding it difficult to keep the farm going. Evangeline had come to love Ben very deeply. Not only was he a good husband to her, but he'd become such a loving father to Hope. In fact, Hope was very close to her step-father. Evangeline had always wanted to have a child with Ben, but their attempts had led to miscarriages until now. Evangeline reveled in the happiness she felt at that moment. She was pregnant for the first time in a number of years. She prayed that the child in her womb would go full term. She couldn't wait to tell Ben. She sat on the porch and waited for him to come in from the fields. She sat watching the sun drop lower in the sky. The days were becoming shorter. Fall was coming. That was her favorite time of the year. It not only was a break from the summer heat, but it was to her a reminder of the majesty of God. She saw the colors of the leaves as a manifestation of His glory. She reflected, as she sat, on how good God had been to her. She had had a young husband who had been her best friend. Sorrow came over her as she wished they had had more time to grow as husband and wife. A smile slowly returned to her face as she reminisced about her last several years with Ben. He was such a blessing, she thought again. Then there was her daughter Hope who'd grown up to be a beautiful young lady. They had their moments when their wills clashed, but the wonderful thing was that Ben would intercede and all would be well again. Now, she hoped, another blessing was on its way. As she was lost in that thought, she looked up to see Ben and Mr. Conroy coming in from the fields.

When Ben saw her, he ran the few hundred remaining feet between her and himself. He jumped up onto the porch, picked her up, and held her in his arms.

"Evangeline, my darling, I missed you so much!"

"Oh, Ben, I've missed you too! How was your day?"

"It was good. We're nearly ready to harvest the crops."

By that time Mr. Conroy stepped onto the porch. He tapped Ben on the shoulder and said, "How about you put my daughter-in-law down so I can have a hug."

Ben put Evangeline down and Mr. Conroy gave her a big hug and a kiss on the cheek.

"How are you feeling today, Dad?"

"I'm doing much better. I'm not so achy."

"I'm so glad to hear it! Mom's waiting for you inside."

With that Mr. Conroy went into the house and left Evangeline and Ben on the porch alone. They sat down together on the porch swing.

"Ben, dear, I have something to tell you."

"What is it, my love?"

"I'm expecting."

Ben's beaming face brightened even more. he pulled her closer to himself, and replied, "That's such great news!" He put his strong hand on her belly. "Lord, may we not lose this one," he prayed. Since knowing Evangeline, he'd become a believer, which had made her so happy. "Shouldn't our daughter be home from school soon? Does she know?"

"No, honey, she doesn't. I wanted you to know first."

"How do you think she'll take the news, Ev?"

"I really don't know, Ben. My relationship has been very difficult with her at times in recent months."

"I'm sure it's just because she's in her teen years and becoming her own person."

"Maybe you should tell her. She might accept the news more freely from you. She adores you."

"She loves you too, Ev."

"I know, but sometimes it doesn't feel that way."

As they were talking, Evangeline saw her daughter walking down the lane, coming home from school. "Honey, here she comes now. You tell her."

"No, you are her mother. You should tell her. I'll be right here with you."

"Oh, alright, my wise husband, I'll tell her."

As Hope reached the porch, she said, "Hi, you two. What's up? You look like you're having a serious conversation."

"Well Hope, honey," Evangeline said, "we have something to tell you. It's really good news!"

"Like I don't have to go to school anymore?"

"Very funny, young lady," said Ben.

"Sweetheart, we're expecting a baby!"

Hope scrunched up her nose and rolled her eyes. "Oh no, you can't be serious! Your timing couldn't be worse! You don't spend much time with me now. You never have. I really need a mother right now. I'll never have you to myself."

Ben shot back at her, "You're not allowed to talk to your mother that way. And you know that's not true."

"What do you know! You're out in the fields most of the day."

"And you're in school most of the day, young lady," replied Ben.

"You two just don't understand!" Hope said and ran into the house.

"Well, that went real well," said Evangeline.

"I'll go in and talk with her," Ben answered and went into the house.

Evangeline sat back down on the porch swing and began to cry. She knew she was reaping the bad fruit of being away from Hope so much when Hope was a young child. She prayed to the Lord to help her right that wrong.

After a little while Ben returned to the porch. He sat down next to Evangeline and put an arm around her. "I know what's wrong. Hope opened up to me just now. She is beginning to see some of her cousins at school a lot. She feels she cannot socialize with them but desperately wants to. She knows the rest of the family is at odds with you but is trying to be respectful of you. She's really torn."

"This is my fault, Ben!"

"No, my love, this is your father's fault."

"He started this, I know. But I'm supposed to be a Christian. I need to make this right."

"You've tried to do so. He wouldn't listen. He could've killed you! I won't let you near him!"

"I have to, Ben, for my daughter's sake. I have to do it for the sake of our two families. The war has kept us divided for too long."

"I'm against this, Ev, but I won't tell you that you can't do it. I don't think you should do this alone, however."

"I have no intention of doing that, my love. We're going to go as a family. I'm going to complete what I started years ago. First, I must go talk to Hope." Evangeline went straight into the house to Hope's room. She knocked on the door. "Can I come in, honey? I have something I want to tell you. I know what's bothering you. I have a plan to make it right. Will you let me talk to you about it?"

"Why should I? How can you make it right after all these years? The family wants nothing to do with us! They consider us traitors. It's not fair! What've I done?"

"You've done nothing. This is a result of grandpa's bitterness. He felt betrayed by your father, and thus, also me. Would you come with me to the attic? I want to show you something."

"What's up there of any importance?"

"I found some letters up there that I thought were lost years ago. They're letters from your father to me. Grandma Conroy hid them there. She couldn't bring herself to get rid of them. Would you like to read them?"

Hope was quiet for a short time, and then slowly opened her door. "Yes, mom, I would like to read them."

Evangeline took Hope by the hand and led her up to the attic. When they arrived there, she pulled the little chest out from behind the books where they were hidden. She opened the chest and handed Hope the first letter. Hope opened the envelope and began to read. By the end of the letter she was crying, but Evangeline handed her the second one, and then a third. As she finished the third letter, Hope said, "I'm sorry, mom. Daddy really loved you."

"Yes, he did. And I really loved him. That's why I made the commitment I did. I did it to bring honor to you father's name, especially after grandpa called him a traitor. Your father and I were very saddened by the war and the way it split our two families."

"I can see that now, mom. I'm so sorry I judged you. I was wrong."

"Will you come with me, with Ben, and grandma and grandpa to Grandpa Ulster's house?"

"Yes, mom, when will we go?"

"Tomorrow's Saturday. We'll go in the morning."

The next morning, right after the sun had come up, Evangeline, Ben, Hope, and Mr. and Mrs. Conroy got into the big wagon and went to the Ulster farm. Evangeline watched the sunlight filtering through the trees as the wagon moved down the road. She thanked God for a bright sunny day. She prayed for the words and wisdom to talk with her father after so many years.

After a short time they arrived at the Ulster farm. Evangeline was very anxious. She wasn't even sure how healthy her father was. The last time she had seen him, he was only a shell of the man he'd been. As the wagon pulled up in front of the very familiar farmhouse, she watched her aunt Audrey emerge from the house.

As the wagon came to a halt, Audrey said, "Girl, what're you doing here? You know your father doesn't want to see you. And what are those no good Conroys doing here? You shouldn't have brought them!"

"Aunt Audrey, my father's going to see me! Bring him down to the big tree by the creek. He'll know which one it is. Have as many cousins of mine that are here come too," replied Evangeline and began walking to the tree where she and Liam had met.

Audrey yelled, "Why should I do that?"

"Tell him I'm going to let him finish what he started years ago."

Ben said, "Are you crazy?"

"What did he try to do?" asked Hope.

"He tried to kill your mother," answered Mr. Conroy.

"Mom, I'm afraid."

"Don't worry, dear Hope," replied Evangeline. "He didn't succeed before, and he won't now, unless God allows it."

They waited for about half an hour and her father didn't appear. At that point Ben said, "He's not coming. Let's go home."

"No, my love, we need to wait a little longer," answered Evangeline. Then they waited about 20 minutes more.

"Ben's right, Evangeline, your father's not coming," said Mr. Conroy.

Just as Evangeline was about to concede that they were right, her father and several cousins appeared. "Why'd you come here with those Conroys?" he said.

"Father," Evangeline said, "has your bitterness not caused enough casualties? You killed mother, tried to shoot me, have never seen your granddaughter, and will soon miss out on coming to know another grandchild. You had to spend time in prison. Haven't you witnessed enough pain? Can't you see that we're not your enemies? The hatred caused by the war has been the foe to all of us. Isn't it time we stopped allowing it to be the victor over us? It has stolen much of what we held dear from us. Are you going to continue to allow that?"

Mr. Ulster looked at his daughter intently for several seconds, and then his eyes moved to gaze upon Hope. He began to quiver, fell to his knees, and began to cry. "I didn't mean to kill your mother. I'm so sorry. I can't live with the guilt of it anymore. I don't want to lose another day with my granddaughter. I don't want to hate my friends, the Conroys.

Josh and Abigail can you forgive a very foolish old man? I turned my whole family against yours and my daughter for a war that has done nothing but rob me of time with those I love. I love you, Evangeline."

Evangeline ran over to him, knelt down beside him, and threw her arms around him. As they both cried, holding tightly to one another, Evangeline looked up into the tree where she and Liam had laid together so many times. The leaves were turning a pinkish red. Autumn had begun and her family's wounds could heal. The war that had plagued her for so long had finally come to an end.

www.ingramcontent.com/pod-product-compliance
Ingram Content Group UK Ltd.
Pitfield, Milton Keynes, MK11 3LW, UK
UKHW041950230426
12048UKWH00008B/247